Quinn was so close— so pulverizingly male.

It took everything Kerry had left not to turn and lay her head against his strong, broad shoulder. Somehow, she knew Quinn could handle big loads and responsibility. He was built for it not only physically, but emotionally, too.

As he stepped away, Kerry keenly felt the loss of his nearness, his care. Opening her eyes, she fell captive to the smoky blueness now banked in his gaze as he studied her in the silence strung between them. For the first time in years Kerry felt another stirring deep within her heart and lower body; it was the stirring of desire for a man. For Quinn Grayson. Even though he was a tough, no-nonsense marine, he had an incredibly surprising and wonderfully tender side, too. It was a beautiful discovery for Kerry.

Because right now she needed someone exactly like Quinn....

* * *

Don't miss next month's installment! *Protecting His Own* is available in Intimate Moments in November—IM #1185.

Dear Reader,

What makes readers love Silhouette Romance? Fans who have sent mail and participated on our www.eHarlequin.com community bulletin boards say they enjoy the heart-thumping emotion, the noble strength of the heroines, the truly heroic nature of the men—all in a quick yet satisfying read. I couldn't have said it better!

This month we have some fantastic series for you. Bestselling author Lindsay McKenna visits use with *The Will To Love* (SR 1618), the latest in her thrilling cross-line adventure MORGAN'S MERCENARIES: ULTIMATE RESCUE. Jodi O'Donnell treats us with her BRIDGEWATER BACHELORS title, *The Rancher's Promise* (SR 1619), about sworn family enemies who fight the dangerous attraction sizzling between them.

You must pick up *For the Taking* (SR 1620) by Lilian Darcy. In this A TALE OF THE SEA, the last of the lost royal siblings comes home. And if that isn't dramatic enough, in Valerie Parv's *Crowns and a Cradle* (SR 1621), part of THE CARRAMER LEGACY, a struggling single mom discovers she's a princess!

Finishing off the month are Myrna Mackenzie's *The Billionaire's Bargain* (SR 1622)—the second book in the latest WEDDING AUCTION series—about a most tempting purchase. And *The Sheriff's 6-Year-Old Secret* (SR 1623) is Donna Clayton's tearjerker.

I hope you enjoy this month's selection. Be sure to drop us a line or visit our Web site to let us know what we're doing right—and any particular favorite topics you want to revisit. Happy reading!

Mary-Theresa Hussey

Mary-Theresa Hussey
Senior Editor

Please address questions and book requests to:
Silhouette Reader Service
U.S.: 3010 Walden Ave., P.O. Box 1325, Buffalo, NY 14269
Canadian: P.O. Box 609, Fort Erie, Ont. L2A 5X3

Lindsay McKenna

THE WILL TO LOVE

SILHOUETTE Romance®
Published by Silhouette Books
America's Publisher of Contemporary Romance

To the innocent and brave men, women and children
who lost their lives on 9-11-01.
You will be in our hearts and memory forever.

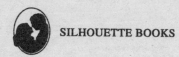 SILHOUETTE BOOKS

ISBN 0-373-19618-0

THE WILL TO LOVE

Copyright © 2002 by Lindsay McKenna

This edition published by arrangement with Harlequin Books S.A.

® and TM are trademarks of Harlequin Books S.A., used under license. Trademarks indicated with ® are registered in the United States Patent and Trademark Office, the Canadian Trade Marks Office and in other countries.

Visit Silhouette at www.eHarlequin.com

Printed in U.S.A.

Books by Lindsay McKenna

LINDSAY McKENNA

A homeopathic educator, Lindsay teaches at the Desert Institute of Classical Homeopathy in Phoenix, Arizona. When she isn't teaching alternative medicine, she is writing books about love. She feels love is the single greatest healer in the world and hopes that her books touch her readers' hearts.

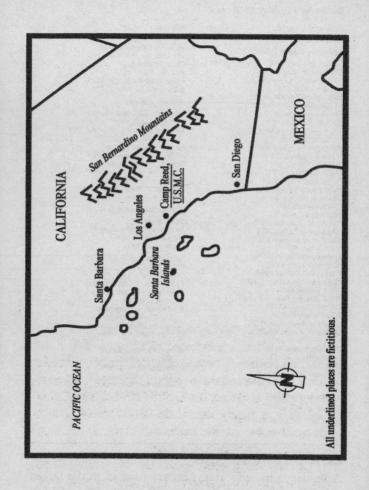

All underlined places are fictitious.

Chapter One

January 14: 0545

It was a bad day getting worse by the moment, Corporal Quinn Grayson decided as he eased out of the dark green Humvee once it stopped against the curb. Above him towered the massive, dark gray concrete headquarters building for U.S. Marine Corps Camp Reed. It was barely dawn, the sky lightening to a pale gold color on the eastern horizon as he took the concrete steps two at a time.

The only thing good about the day was that he was going to see someone in Logistics whom he truly admired and respected: Morgan Trayhern, who was a living hero to the Marine Corps. Feeling his mood lifting slightly, Quinn wove in and around the crowds of swiftly moving personnel, all dressed similarly to himself in desert-colored utilities. The helmet on his head always felt heavy, and he was glad to take it off as he stepped through the double doors and into the building itself.

The noise level inside was low, but the faces of the office pogues were filled with stress and anxiety as they hurried like bees in a stirred-up hive. The H.Q. was organized chaos, Quinn decided. And why wouldn't it be? Two weeks ago the worst earthquake in American history had turned the Los Angeles basin upside down and inside out. Millions of helpless victims desperately needed food, water and medicine. Worse, there were no highways left into the basin; they had all been destroyed by the massive quake.

The only way in and out now was by helicopter. From the platoon he was assigned to assist in the emergency operations, Quinn saw only the tip of the iceberg as far as rescue efforts to the civilian populace went. Yesterday evening he'd been in the loading area with his platoon, piling food, water and medicine into the choppers, when his sergeant, Sean O'Hara, had ordered him to go see Morgan at 0600.

Turning now, Quinn headed up the stairs to the second floor, where Logistics, the heart and brains of Operation Sky Lift, was located, and where Morgan had an office. En route Quinn passed a number of office types descending rapidly, their hands filled with files and, more than likely, orders.

Pushing the stairwell door open and striding forward, Quinn located Morgan's office halfway down the passageway, which was also crowded with busy personnel. Tension was high; he could feel it. Shrugging his broad shoulders, as if to rid himself of the accumulated stress he felt in the building, Quinn halted in front of the open door and rapped once with his knuckles. Morgan Trayhern was behind the green metal desk, head down, writing a set of orders for a woman officer in a flight uniform. Quinn saw the black wing insignia sewn into the fabric of her suit and knew instantly that she was probably a helo pilot.

Morgan lifted his head. His scowl faded. "Quinn! Great, you're here. Come in." He raised his hand and beckoned him into the office. "I'll be just a moment."

"Yes, sir," Quinn said. He took a step inside and stood at attention. The woman pilot, a Marine Corps captain, nodded toward him.

"Ma'am. Good morning."

"Good morning, Corporal. At ease, please," she said.

Quinn nodded and relaxed into an at-ease stance behind her, near the wall. "Yes, ma'am."

"You had coffee yet, Quinn?" Morgan rumbled

as he signed the second and third sets of orders before him.

"No, sir." Quinn kept his helmet, which was splotched with desert camouflage colors of yellow, brown and gray, beneath his left elbow and against his hip. He noticed Morgan was dressed in civilian attire—jeans and a red, long-sleeved cotton shirt with the cuffs rolled up to just below his elbows. He looked out of place in the marine-green office.

Gesturing to his right, Morgan said with a grin, "Grab a cup of java, then. I managed to scrounge up my very own coffeemaker. A rarity, you know. Help yourself, Son."

Quinn smiled slightly and moved toward the machine. "Yes, sir. Thank you, sir."

Blowing out a breath of air, Morgan put the pen aside and gave the thick set of orders to the helicopter pilot. "There you go, Captain Jackson. Congratulations. You and your copilot are now responsible for Area Six. We've transferred the other team to Area Five.

"Yes, sir. Thank you, sir. We'll do a good job."

Morgan smiled up at her. Captain Jackson was in her middle twenties, with short black hair, intense gray eyes and a sincere face that was currently filled with excitement. H.Q. had just gotten a whole new batch of helicopter pilots transferred in yesterday from other Marine Corps bases around the U.S. Having new pilots on board would give the hardworking helo crews stationed at Camp Reed a desperate and much-needed rest from the twelve-hour days they'd been putting in for the last two weeks. Pilots could fly only so long without sufficient rest and recoup time before they began making critical mistakes. Jackson was one of many personnel scheduled to come to Morgan's office today for orders.

"Good luck out there, Captain." Morgan rose. "And be careful, you hear? Things are unstable right now. We've already had a helicopter crew murdered by a survivalist group in Area Five."

She came to attention. "Yes, sir, we'll be careful. Thank you, sir."

"Dismissed," Morgan murmured. He stood and watched the woman, who was nearly six feet tall, big boned and athletic, turn on her heel and quickly march out the door. Swiveling his head, Morgan gave Quinn Grayson a warm look. The corporal had just poured a cup of coffee. Moving to the machine, Morgan poured himself one, too.

"Come with me, Quinn. Now is about the only time today I might get to see Laura. You remember my wife?"

"Yes, sir, I do." He sipped the coffee tentatively. It was fresh and hot, and he savored it. "She's here, too?" How could that be? Quinn knew Laura lived in Montana, near the headquarters Morgan kept for Perseus in Philipsburg. Quinn and his fire team had been selected to be part of two different Perseus rescue missions in Iraq, where pilots were that had been shot down in the No Fly Zone earlier in the year. He and his team had been flown back to the secret headquarters in Philipsburg, an out-of-the-way place only a few tourists and trout fishermen found in the summer. It was a perfect hiding spot, Quinn had thought. He'd met Morgan's lovely blond-haired wife there by accident, when she'd brought over recently baked cookies for all of them. It was a thoughtful gesture that was as surprising as it was unexpectedly generous. Quinn had relished his share of the chocolate-chip cookies, and so had his grateful men. He had found Laura to be beautiful, elegant and sensitive. Quinn thought Morgan was the luckiest man in the world to have a wife like that. Cookies during a briefing. He'd never get that in the Marine Corps. No, he liked working with Morgan and Perseus. But he wondered how Morgan's wife had wound up in the midst of this disaster.

"We were at a hotel in south Los Angeles, celebrating New Year, when the quake hit," Morgan explained as they left the office and headed down the stairs. "Laura was trapped in wreckage." At the bottom of the stairs, Morgan pushed open the door. Gesturing toward the end of the passageway, he took quick strides toward it. Quinn, who was six foot tall, and shorter than Morgan, had to lengthen his stride to keep up with him.

"Your wife was trapped?" he asked with a scowl as they moved out the doors and into the brightening day. The sun was going to rise soon and already the darkness of the night had fled.

"Yeah," Morgan muttered. "Thank goodness a Marine Corps rescue officer and her dog located Laura."

"Is she all right, sir?" They hurried down the stairs toward the hospital a block away. The world around them was already in high gear. The shrieking whine of jets at the nearby airport filled the air, along with the deeper chugging sounds of diesel truck convoys loaded with supplies lumbering across the base. A whole fleet of helicopters were taking off one by one, hotfooting it out of Camp Reed with the first supplies of the day for desperate people across the disaster area.

Quinn drew abreast of Morgan as he walked swiftly toward the hospital.

"Laura suffered a broken ankle. She had surgery here. Then, shortly after the surgery, she developed a blood clot. They had to string up her leg with a pulley, and she was tied down like a roping calf." Morgan grinned wryly. "My wife is not one to lie in bed all day and do nothing. We had to wait until some blood-thinning drugs were flown in from Seattle for her." He rubbed his hands together. "Today, she gets out of her contraption and into a wheelchair. The doctor says the clot is dissolved and her ankle is stable enough for her to be a little more active.''

''Almost two weeks in a bed would drive me nuts,'' Quinn muttered. It would. He was restless by nature, and loved the outdoors and the strenuous activity demanded of marines.

''Yes, well…'' Morgan chuckled ''…if it hadn't been for a tiny baby the team rescued from beneath the rubble, Laura would never have survived bed rest. She's been taking care of Baby Jane Fielding for the nurses. And the hospital staff bring up other infants so Laura can hold them and bottle-feed them. They've been keeping her busy.''

Quinn smiled knowingly. There was no doubt about Laura's maternal side. He liked that about women in general, although in his world, he saw mostly women marines, with tough, demanding jobs. Still, he saw that nurturing side in many of them, too. It was something he enjoyed about women, in or out of the service.

They hurried into the chaotic, busy hospital and up an elevator. Quinn was glad to escape the bustle once they arrived at the private room where Laura Trayhern sat in her wheelchair, an infant wrapped in a pink blanket in her arms.

''Hello, Quinn.'' Laura greeted him warmly as he approached. ''You look well.''

''Thank you, ma'am,'' he said, nodding to her and smiling. The infant was suckling strongly on a bottle of milk. "I'm glad to hear from Mr. Trayhern that you're doing okay."

"I'm fine." Laura lifted her face toward Morgan as he bent and gave her a kiss on the brow. Then he gently stroked the baby's dark, soft hair.

Quinn saw the man's face change remarkably. For a moment, he glimpsed the love burning in Morgan's eyes for his wife of many years. And when Morgan ran his fingertips caressingly across the baby's hair, Quinn saw tenderness replace his normally stoic expression. But as Morgan's fingers lifted away, Quinn saw the same hard mask fall back into place. Despite that, there was no doubt in his mind that Morgan loved his wife and the orphaned baby.

"Come over here, Son. Let's sit down and go over this new plan that you're going to initiate for the basin."

Moving to the two metal chairs near the venetian-blind-covered window, Quinn excused himself from Laura. Morgan handed him one of two red folders and sat down. Opening his copy, Quinn saw a set of signed orders with his name at the top. The other members of his fire team were named, as well.

Scowling, Morgan studied the folder opened in his lap. "We're initiating a basin-wide plan B today, and you're a part of that effort—you and your fire team. It's a trial balloon. A work in progress, so to speak. We don't know if it will work or not, so you're an experiment of sorts. We can't afford to put a full squad of ten men into each area. Camp Reed doesn't have the personnel to pull that off. But by splitting up a squad into two fire teams of five people each, plus their leader, we have a chance to do something rather than nothing.'' He looked squarely at Quinn. ''So you're it. You're our test case. You're to play it by ear and see where the energy flows in this changing situation. You're the only fire team we're putting in there for now. If it works, we'll insert others later.''

''Five marines in each given area?'' Quinn asked.

''That's right. We've divided the basin into twelve quadrants. These are huge blocks of real estate. We're talking ten to twenty square miles, depending upon the location, the population of the area and so on.'' Scratching his head, Morgan gave Quinn a rueful look. ''Believe me, Logistics has been wrestling with this nightmare. The basin has no law enforcement. Without backup, the police in some areas can't do what they've been trained to do. There are no highways to drive on to get to a problem area. They're pretty much limited to handling problems within walking distance of their base of operation.''

Morgan pulled a sheet of fax paper from his file folder and handed it to Quinn. ''This is Deputy Sheriff Kerry Chelton. She is the only surviving member of the law enforcement agency in Area

Five. Kerry contacted us by radio a week ago, and I've had the pleasure of talking with this young woman a number of times. Damned intelligent and resourceful. She found a gasoline generator, some fuel, and managed to retrieve a radio from the sheriff's building, which collapsed and killed everyone inside it. She calls us every night with reports. Beautiful woman, isn't she?''

Taking the paper, Quinn saw the photo on it. For no explainable reason, his heart contracted instantly. The black-and-white picture showed a woman with dark hair, cut to just below her ears. With her heart-shaped face, full but compressed lips and wide eyes, she was a very attractive woman, Quinn decided. The head shot showed her in her law enforcement uniform. The resolve in her large eyes was obvious. She exuded confidence.

''Yes, sir, she's a looker, no doubt,'' he murmured.

''Kerry has been in regular contact with our radio group at H.Q. She's been helping us formulate stage two of our rescue efforts.'' Sighing, Morgan said in a low voice, ''There's a lot of people out there dying right now. We just can't get to them soon enough. The water mains are broken, so there's no fresh water supply, or at least, not enough for the millions that are trapped out there. And food, while less of a problem now because people can go to their homes and eat whatever canned goods they find, will be disappearing shortly, too. Kerry has been scouting as much of Area Five as she can every day and giving us nightly reports. She's telling us what the needs are, and we've been trying to organize community groups in each area to help stabilize the situation. We're trying to find local police, state troopers, sheriff's deputies—anyone in law enforcement—to become the hub of this wheel we're building. Without law and order, chaos continues.''

''Yes, sir, I've been hearing plenty about that gang in Area Five.''

''Humph. Those survivalists. They call themselves Diablo—or Devil. And you, Quinn, are going to be taking them on.'' Morgan gave him a hard look.

''I'd like nothing better, sir. They killed two marine pilots in cold blood. That's reason enough to go after them.'' At the thought, anger tightened his chest. Yet when Quinn studied Kerry's photo again, his heart sped up and thumped violently for a beat or two. Part of him was eager to meet this inventive woman. Another more prejudiced part of him didn't believe a woman could be *that* resourceful. Yet Morgan obviously admired and respected her, so she had to have the right stuff. In Quinn's experience, women were not especially handy or practical. Nurturing others was one thing, but there really wasn't much place for that in the Marine Corps. And he really didn't like the integration of females into male slots in the corps. Not at all.

"At 0800, Quinn, you are to go to LZ Echo with your fire team. The pilots of that Huey will take you and your team into Area Five. They're going to drop you at a destroyed shopping mall parking lot. Deputy Chelton will meet you there. She has a makeshift H.Q. set up nearby with that generator. What she needs now is help." Morgan eyed him with a slight, twisted smile. "Firepower, in other words."

"And who's in charge, sir?"

"Both of you will be."

Quinn frowned. "But sir, to run an operation like this…going after Diablo…why should a civilian have *any* say over what we do?" He struggled with his choice of words and tone of voice. The term *civilian* had sounded disrespectful. Instantly, he was sorry for how he'd framed his objection.

Trayhern's face darkened, and his blue eyes turned icy for a moment. "Listen to me, Quinn. That woman just lost everyone she ever cared about two weeks ago. Most people would be so stunned with such grief and loss they couldn't think straight. Kerry has single-handedly set up a base of operations for Area Five. She has tracked Diablo. She's been like Lara Croft, Princess Xena and Supergirl all wrapped into one. Without her constant input, her observations and suggestions from the field, we wouldn't be launching this second phase so soon.

She's been able to help us define what is needed out there.

"Your fire team was chosen because you have emergency medical training. We're desperate for medical intervention out there. Without Kerry's guidance, we couldn't have formulated this concept we're starting to put together to help the folks. Your team is an experiment. If it works, we'll do more of it."

Stung by Morgan's censure, Quinn lowered his gaze and looked at the file. Kerry's photo stared back at him. She wasn't smiling, but she had a softness about her face. Her nose was thin and fine. Her eyes were far apart, her gaze clear and direct. Swallowing hard, Quinn nodded. "Yes, sir, I hear you."

"Don't go in there with a chip on your shoulder about women," Morgan warned him in a growl. "The last thing I need on this mission is a man who's prejudiced about what women can or can't do." He reached out and tapped Kerry's picture. "She's the kind of woman I like to hire for Perseus. Kerry thinks on her feet. She's creative. Trustworthy. And she doesn't miss anything. Maybe it's because of her training in law enforcement, but she has an eye for details. And without her input, Quinn, we would be up a creek right now. She's just about the only one out there who has radio contact with Camp Reed. Ask yourself how she managed to jury-rig that. No, I think she's one hell of a person. And

I want you to go into this assignment with that same attitude.''

Chastened, Quinn felt his heart contract when Morgan called Kerry trustworthy. Maybe he was still feeling the pain of his breakup with Frannie Walton, a civilian secretary he'd met in Oceanside nearly two years ago. Since then, he'd had a lot of trouble trusting any woman. After the way Frannie had treated him, he'd crawled into a dark hole of hurt, his pride wounded. She'd been a social climber and on an emotional level, Frannie had been anything but reliable or trustworthy. Quinn had been raised in the backwoods country of Kentucky, where women were still women. They didn't try and take a man's job away from him. Nope, they were good wives, raised kids and stayed home to cook, clean and be mothers.

Rubbing his chest above his heart, Quinn tried to pay attention as Morgan explained what was expected of him and his fire team.

''You're to set up an H.Q. with Kerry. She's your civilian liaison or counterpart. Without her, you'd be a duck out of water. She knows the turf, the people and the area. Twenty-seven years old and a graduate of law enforcement, she was on the fast track in the sheriff's department.

''Right now, Kerry needs help in continuing to organize the people, to keep peace and to stop the slide into chaos that's happening more and more.

People are desperate. They need water, and are willing to steal from others to get it. Kerry is trying her best to locate a well in her area, but so far, no luck. Even if they do find one, there's no guarantee it will have clean water, given the lack of sewage facilities."

"Our mission, then," Quinn murmured, "is threefold, right? We're to try and hunt down Diablo and corral them. We're to help Kerry Chelton set up an H.Q. And lastly, we're to help organize the area so it doesn't disintegrate into turf wars over water and food?"

"You got it," Morgan said, satisfaction vibrating in his voice. "Now, you may find that one of those three takes priority. We don't know which one that might be yet, so be flexible and let this thing evolve as the situation develops. Kerry has been working hard for two weeks to set up some kind of organized response. She's been instrumental in bringing civilians together and getting them to work with one another. What she needs is muscle. And that's where you and your team come in. You're military, and people will respect that more than anything. With Diablo ranging across Kerry's area, people are going ballistic. Your presence alone should help calm a lot of fears." Morgan turned to another page in his file.

"The Diablo have an MO—modus operandi—of going into a house they think might have a stash of food or water. They move in small groups, maybe

one to four men. The men talk with the house owners, pretending to be part of the rescue effort, and
ask if they have children." Morgan's voice deepened with fury. "If the answer is yes, one member
will find and hold the child hostage, at gunpoint.
Then the rest of the pack come out of hiding and
ransack the house for food, water, money, jewelry.
The home owners are helpless. They can't stop
them. They don't want their children hurt. To date,
Diablo have already killed five people, not including
the two Marine Corps pilots. They don't tolerate any
rebellion by anyone."

"They shoot first and ask questions later," Quinn
muttered, anger stirring in him again. It was one
thing to prey on adults, quite another to involve innocent children. His mouth flattened. Right now,
he'd like nothing better than to get his hands on the
leader of that gang.

"Exactly."

"Do you know who's heading up Diablo?"

"No, but Kerry thinks she knows and is trying to
piece it together for us. She's been trying to shadow
their movements."

"That's dangerous."

"Sure it is," Moran agreed, "but she's fearless,
that woman. She's been tailing them without their
knowledge whenever she gets a chance. She calls in
their last position, and that helps us keep tabs on
them, and to protect helicopter crews flying into that

area. Right now, it's a cat-and-mouse game. We keep changing our landing area to outwit Diablo and get basic goods to the civilians. And on days when she can't detect them in Area Five, the helo goes back to the original LZ, which is her H.Q. set up at the destroyed shopping center. That's where you'll be flown into today.'' Morgan's mouth quirked. ''But that'll go only so far. What we need is the gang captured and extricated. We've got a brig cell waiting for those bastards.''

''Then you've come to the right team, sir. We'll find them and be Thor's hammer to 'em.''

Grinning sourly, Morgan studied the marine, whose face was dark with anger and set with determination. ''Thor's hammer'' was an old saying in the corps. Morgan could recall many times when, as young officers during the Vietnam War, he and his friends at an officers' club would toast to Odin, Norse king of the gods. The Norse god of thunder, Thor, hurled thunderbolts at his enemies. Yes, Quinn was no doubt going to be Thor's ''hammer''—his lightning bolt—in this situation. Morgan had full confidence in him.

''We're counting heavily on you, Quinn. You've worked twice with me on important missions and I know you're a warrior at heart. You have the medical background. If anyone can track down Diablo, you can. You come from Kentucky hill people, and they're the best hunters and trackers in the business.

That's one of the reasons I chose you—you're one hell of a bird dog on a scent.''

Laughing shortly, Quinn nodded. "Yes, sir, I am."

Morgan straightened and placed his hands over the file. "Just try to get along with Deputy Chelton, okay? That's the one fly in this ointment. I know you'd rather work with men. That's your background and I understand that. But Kerry is exceptional, Quinn, and I feel you two will make a hell a team. Dodge is infested with bad guys, so to speak, and she needs some muscle to help get them out of there.''

"Then you've come to the right person, sir." Quinn felt a lethal resolve flow through him as he met and held Morgan's deep blue gaze. "We won't let you down. My team and I have been together nearly two years. We know each other's thoughts, and we've been battle tested. I want Diablo more than most, sir. I don't believe in using children as shields. That's unforgivable.''

"It is," Morgan agreed unhappily. "Everyone's traumatized by the quake. Having these survivalists roving around and adding to the chaos, endangering and scaring children and killing adults, isn't acceptable. We all need to pull together, work together in order to survive this nightmare.''

"I'll try my best to work with Deputy Chelton,''

he promised Morgan. More than anything, Quinn
wanted Morgan's respect.

"Do your best, Corporal Grayson. She's an exceptional woman, not to mention a savvy police officer. We're lucky to have her." Morgan held out
his hand. "Good luck, Quinn, to you and your men.
Get your gear together, take this set of orders and
hotfoot it out to LZ Echo for an 0800 takeoff.
Kerry's expecting you."

As Morgan shook his hand, Quinn tried to ignore
the photo of Kerry Chelton resting in his lap on the
opened file. A woman. What bad luck. Somehow,
though, Quinn would try to make the best of it. Was
she another Frannie? A social climber? Could he
trust this Kerry Chelton?

His emotions smarted at those unanswered questions. Where he'd grown up, women didn't become
police officers. They were wives and mothers and
that was it.

And he was going to jump from the frying pan
into the fire today. Figuring out how much or little
he could trust Chelton would be his first order of
business. Until he knew that, they were technically
all at risk, and Quinn wasn't about to get his head
shot off because some woman was involved in the
plan.

No, he'd go in distrusting her completely.

Chapter Two

January 14: 0830

For the first time since the earthquake, Kerry Chelton felt hope. It wasn't much more than a thin, fragile thread, but it began to take root in her traumatized heart and lifted her flagging spirits. Dressed in the dark green slacks and tan, long-sleeved blouse that was her sheriff's deputy uniform, a silver badge over her left pocket, she stood at the ready on the massive asphalt parking lot of the destroyed shopping center as she watched two U.S. Marine Corps helicopters landing.

A sudden, unexpected sense of joy enveloped her. She was getting help. Help! Oh, how badly she needed some.

Putting her hands up to protect her eyes from flying debris kicked up by the rotors, she surveyed the
group of twenty people standing around her. Patient
and respectful, as they were waiting eagerly for the
first Huey, which was carrying a crucial supply of
bottled water, to land. The water would be distributed at the other end of the shopping complex,
where Kerry had had her people build a makeshift
depot out of bricks and other material taken from
destroyed buildings. On other days, when Diablo
was "active" in her area, Kerry would redirect the
helo to a safer LZ. The supplies would be distributed
from that location instead. This morning there had
been no activity with Diablo, so the original LZ was
put into use.

Her gaze moved to the second Huey, which she
knew was bearing the five marines Morgan Trayhern
had sent. Morgan had been her lifeline since she'd
cobbled the generator and radio together. His deep,
soothing voice over the radio day after day had
given her hope and kept her sanity intact. Now he
had sent her reinforcements to help keep Area Five
stable. Morgan had spoken enthusiastically of the
leader of this fire team, Corporal Quinn Grayson,
who was a marine as well as an EMT. God knew,
Area Five needed medical intervention! She could
hardly wait to meet him.

Deep within her, Kerry knew she was still pulverized by shock because of the recent traumatic

events. She had felt nothing, emotionally, for two weeks. Now a trickle of hope wound through her pounding heart as the Huey with the marines landed within two hundred feet of her. Kerry spread her feet apart in order to remain standing against the buffeting wind. As the Huey powered down, she saw the door slide open.

The first marine to jump down had to be Quinn Grayson, Kerry decided. She could tell by the authority in his stance that he was the leader. Tall and broad-shouldered, he clutched an M-16 in his hands as he warily looked around. When he turned and snapped an order, four more marines disembarked, on guard and alert.

Instantly, as she watched him walk away from the helicopter and eye the knot of people around her, Kerry liked Grayson. He was looking for her, she knew. She was his contact. Stepping forward, she saw him halt and stare at her assessingly. Was she friend or enemy? Pain in the butt or help? Her heart fluttered wildly in her chest for a moment. That was an odd reaction, Kerry thought, as she walked quickly toward him.

She hadn't smiled in two weeks, but she did now—a smile of welcome, but also of relief. Although she could carry a heavy load on her broad-shouldered five-foot-eleven frame, this disaster had stressed her out completely. And Grayson looked strong, capable and powerful as he stood there look-

ing at her through narrowed, dark blue eyes. Kerry
felt his gaze move over her as she closed the distance between them. Behind her, she heard the foot-
steps of her volunteers as they moved toward the
other Huey. As usual, they would carry the boxes
of precious water to the "store" at the other end of
the shopping center for distribution.

As Kerry drew within ten feet of Quinn, her heart
soared unexpectedly, with such a rush of happiness
that it shook her completely. The marine had an oval
face with a firm-looking chin. Though his lips were
thinned, she could see he had a wide mouth, with
laugh lines deeply indented at each corner. His nose
was long and straight, the nostrils flaring as she approached, as if to pick up her scent. He seemed as
much wild animal as human to her, and yet the quality of danger surrounding Grayson made Kerry feel
secure for the first time since the quake. This marine
knew how to protect; she could feel it in her bones.
His black brows made dark slashes above his glittering blue gaze. The color of his eyes reminded
Kerry of the glacial ice up in Alaska, where she'd
taken a cruise with her now deceased husband, Lee
Chelton. The color was most unusual—almost un-
earthly—and Kerry thought it looked like the color
of heaven, such was its ethereal beauty. Quinn's pu-
pils were large and black, and she saw intelligence
gleaming there, as well as surprise. Why the sur-

prise? she wondered, as she lifted her hand to wave, her mouth pulling into a relieved smile.

"Corporal Grayson? I'm Kerry Chelton. Welcome to our little corner of the world."

During the helo flight in Area Five, Quinn had decided to keep things on a business level and not be very friendly. Now, as the tall, willowy woman in the sheriff's deputy uniform held out her cut, dirty hand, he felt his resolve falter. The black-and-white photo he'd seen of Kerry Chelton had done nothing to prepare him for the woman before him now, her short, tousled brown hair rife with gold highlights as it framed her heart-shaped face. Maybe it was the look of relief in her huge gray eyes that touched his hardened heart. Or, maybe it was the way the corners of her mouth softened and her lower lip trembled as she welcomed him.

Quinn didn't know what magic was at work, but suddenly he transferred his weapon to his left hand and thrust out his right hand to enclose hers. Kerry Chelton looked utterly worn-out. He saw the dark smudges beneath her incredibly beautiful eyes, which now sparkled with unshed tears. Something inside him made him want to open his arms, pull her into them and hold her. The relief in her gaze, the sudden emotion revealed in her dirt-smudged face, got to him. She was melting his armor with her unsure smile and sparkling tears, Quinn thought as he saw her swallow convulsively, struggling to hold back her emotions. Because he'd been so hurt by a woman, Quinn struggled to remain wary. Somehow this woman was opening him up and he had no control over it. The last thing Quinn wanted was to allow himself to get emotionally close to her.

Her hand was warm and firm in his, though he was careful of how much pressure he exerted on her long, slender fingers. Shocked by how dirty she was, he reminded himself that none of these people had water to wash or bathe. Her hair was mussed, in dire need of a comb, shampoo and water.

"I'm Corporal Grayson," he told her, speaking loudly in order to be heard over the shriek of the helicopters.

"Pleased to meet you. Come on, let's go to my 'office.'" She grinned and pointed toward the shopping center. Wild, fleeting tingles ran up her fingers and arm and cascaded into her heart, which was thumping without pause. Grayson's stony persona, combined with the fact that he was a marine, gave her such hope. If the truth was known, Kerry wanted to simply fall into his arms to be held. She knew that wasn't possible—that it was only her knee-jerk reaction in the midst of the shock and trauma—but there was something wonderfully secure about this marine. She'd seen his icy blue eyes turn warm as their hands met in welcome. And the way he'd wrapped his long, strong fingers around hers had made Kerry feel protected and…something else. She couldn't identify the emotion right now, with all the activity going on around her.

Quinn raised his hand in a silent order for his team to follow him as Kerry took the lead. On his left shoulder, a radio was attached to the epaulet of the camouflage jacket he wore over his flak vest. Pressing the button and turning his head to speak into it, he told the helicopter pilots of both birds to lift off, that contact had been made.

The Huey helicopters, flown by Lieutenants Galway and McGregor, had off-loaded the water. The helo's engine changed pitch and, within a minute, lifted off to head back to Camp Reed. Quinn walked with his men spread out behind him like a V of geese following their leader. They each remained on guard, their rifles locked and loaded. Quinn wasn't taking any chances. They were in enemy territory as far as he was concerned. Ahead of them, Kerry walked quickly toward a makeshift structure with a roof that was nothing more than a piece of corrugated tin laid awkwardly on top. The "house" had been painstakingly put together with wire, broken blocks and other material obviously retrieved from the destroyed shopping center. The entire three-story mall, which was at least a quarter mile long, had collapsed. Quinn had not seen this level of destruction yet, and he felt stunned by what the powerful quake had done. It was unimaginable to him. Unthinkable. Horrifying.

Kerry halted in front of the small shack in the midst of the rubble. "This is it, Corporal Grayson." She gestured toward the hovel. "My home." It hurt to say those words. Her real home, a block away from the sheriff's facility, was now nothing but broken brick, shattered glass and a twisted roof.

Quinn halted near Kerry and looked at the structure. There were several yellow wool blankets strung across the front, one serving as a door. Looking around, he saw the team of volunteers trundling the boxes of bottled water toward the other end of the shopping center.

Kerry followed his gaze. "They're taking the water to our distribution center," she told him.

"There's no fighting about who gets what?"

Shaking her head, Kerry said, "Not yet...but people are real desperate, Corporal. Real desperate."

At that moment, a little black-haired girl around seven years old stumbled sleepily from behind the blanketed door. She was dressed in a grungy pink flannel nightgown that showed off her toothpick legs and the red socks on her feet. As the little girl rubbed her sleepy eyes, Kerry instantly moved forward and scooped her up in her arms.

Turning, she said to Grayson, "This is Petula. Her parents are...well, in heaven...." She sent Quinn a pleading look, obviously asking him to play along with her. "I found her trapped in her home and we dug her out ten days ago. Petula stays with me now...."

Mouth turning downward, Quinn watched as Petula, who had shining brown eyes and long black hair, wrapped her thin arms around Kerry's neck and rested her head on her shoulder.

"I'm hungry, Kerry," she whimpered.

"I know, Pet, I know," Kerry soothed, moving her hand gently across the child's tiny shoulders. "I'll see what I can find, okay?"

Quinn's scowl deepened. Like each of his men, he had on an eighty-pound pack filled with food. "I've got an MRE—meal ready to eat—with eggs, bacon and hash browns. How about if I get that warmed up for her?"

Heart expanding, Kerry bit back her tears. "Oh... that would be wonderful!" Relief washed over her as she stood there holding Petula in her arms. Since Kerry had found her, the little girl had cried often, wanting her parents, and Kerry had told her they'd gone to heaven and would watch over her from there. There was no way she would tell Petula that her parents were trapped inside their house, dead. Each day Kerry tried to keep the child busy with small activities, and she slept with her each night after she finished her patrol of the area, keeping her arms wrapped around the little girl to give her a sense of safety in a world gone mad.

Turning, Grayson gave his men orders to spread

out, reconnoiter the entire shopping center area. His fire team consisted of three privates and a lance corporal. He assigned Private Orvil Perkins, a Virginia hill boy, to guard the center against fighting or stealing, and make sure the distribution of water went quickly and quietly. Then he gave LCPL Beau Parish orders to check out the rest of the shopping center with Privates Cliff Ludlow and Lewis Worth. Parish was a North Carolina Eastern Cherokee Indian, and a damn fine tracker and hunter. Right now, Quinn was grateful that his men had been with him nearly two years and could be trusted. They each carried a radio on their left shoulder, so could stay in touch no matter where they were. At the first sign of trouble, Quinn would be notified.

He turned to Kerry. "Do members of the Diablo gang wear any kind of special clothing or symbols so my men might see them coming?"

She nodded. "Yes, they wear white headbands." Grimacing, she whispered, "But they aren't always so obvious. When one or two infiltrate a neighborhood, they look like us." She glanced down at herself and gave a wry grimace. "Unclean and smelly. They only put the headband on after they've taken a hostage."

"I hear you," Quinn muttered with a scowl. "Okay, men, spread out. Be eyes and ears at this stage. Anything odd, call me immediately. I'll be here with Deputy Chelton trying to come up to speed on what we're up against. When you're done with your reconnoiter, come back here. Understand?''

The four marines nodded.

''All except you, Perkins,'' Grayson ordered. ''You stay at the distribution center. Look like you mean business.''

Once his men headed off to follow his orders, Quinn glanced over at Kerry, who was gently kissing Petula's smudged forehead. A sudden, unexpected ache built in him as he watched her full, soft lips caress the child's wrinkled brow. What would it be like to be caressed like that? To capture her mouth beneath his?

His thoughts were so startling, coming as they did during the present situation, that they rocked Quinn completely. On the way here, he'd been mentally trying to shut out Sheriff Deputy Chelton. Well, that was going to be impossible. She was more attractive in real life, even if she was dirty and unkempt. And her natural, womanly warmth reached out and touched him on this cold, windy January morning.

His scowl deepened as he watched her gently rock Petula. The child had her arms around Kerry's neck, her eyes closed as she snuggled tightly beneath her chin. Kerry seemed so very maternal to Quinn in that moment. And when she lifted her dark, thick lashes to look at him, he growled, ''Come on. Let's get this girl and you something decent to eat in there.''

He pointed toward the hovel Kerry called home. The idea that this pile of bricks, broken boards and drywall could be called a shelter left a bad taste in Quinn's mouth. But such were the living conditions for many Americans on this fourteenth day after the killer quake. Thinning his lips, Quinn pulled back the blanket to allow Kerry and the child to enter.

Inside, Grayson locked his rifle and set it down. Under no circumstances did he want Petula fingering the trigger mechanism and firing it off by accident. That would be unthinkable, so he made certain the safety mechanism was secure.

''Have a seat,'' Kerry invited softly, kneeling down on the floor, which she'd covered with some Oriental rugs she'd found at the shopping center. At least they didn't have to sleep on dirt like a lot of other people had to do.

Quinn grunted and went to a corner where he saw a hole dug in the ground, charred bits of wood and ash around it. Shrugging out of his pack, he set it on the floor, careful not to lean it against the rickety wall, which probably wouldn't take its full weight.

''Helluva place you live in,'' he muttered, opening the pack with quick, sure movements.

Kerry raised one eyebrow. ''Corporal? Could you watch your language? This little girl here doesn't need to hear cursing.''

Biting back a reply, he nodded. "Yeah, you're right. Sorry," he replied, glancing uneasily at Kerry, who was sitting cross-legged on the rug, the child in her arms, the girl's head resting against her breast as she sucked her thumb. Kerry was smiling down at Petula and gently threading her fingers through the child's tangled black hair.

"Is this your first time in the basin?" she asked Quinn.

"First time," he answered. He pulled out some food packets. In all, he had twenty. Lining them up in order of breakfast, lunch and dinner, he opened the first one and put a heating tab beneath it to warm it up.

Kerry's mouth watered as the odor of bacon and eggs filled the space. Her stomach clenched in hunger as she watched the marine handle the MRE with deft, sure movements. There was nothing soft or vulnerable about Corporal Grayson. No, he was all-business. The dark look on his face told Kerry a lot. Shock was written in his eyes, even though he tried to hide it from her as he worked quietly.

Taking utensils from his pack, he readied the plate of eggs and bacon. The look on Kerry's face as he handed it to her made him flinch inwardly.

"How long since you ate last?"

Shrugging, Kerry said, "I don't know. I'm so busy, so tired most of the time, that I forget about things like that."

Quinn watched with fascination as she sat Petula in front of her, gave her the warmed tray and placed the fork in her hand. Immediately, the child began stuffing the eggs into her mouth, hot or not.

"Take it easy...." Kerry whispered to Petula. "If you eat too fast, you'll throw it up, honey. And you want to keep down what you're eating. Okay?"

Petula didn't understand how sensitive her hungry, fatigued body could be, so Kerry monitored the amount of food the child took in. Halfway through the unexpected feast, Petula yawned, rubbed her eyes and murmured, "I feel sleepy...."

Setting the plate aside, Kerry smiled gently and eased the girl onto a blanket, beside a stuffed purple dinosaur near her pillow. Getting up on her hands and knees, Kerry drew a second blanket around her and tucked it in.

"Go to sleep, honey. Your stomach is full for the first time in a long time, and all your energy is going there to digest it." She ran her hand soothingly across Petula's thin back, and very soon the child fell asleep, her arms around Barney.

Quinn motioned to the MRE. "Why don't you eat the rest?"

Kerry frowned. "There are so many people out there starving. If I ate it, I'd feel guilty."

"Eat," he ordered, studying the way her blouse hung on her frame. She'd probably dropped a good ten pounds or more in the last two weeks. Seeing the hungry glint in her eyes, Quinn added, "Look, I need you strong, awake and healthy. So dig in, will you?"

Casting him a glance, she picked up the plate and sat down opposite him. "You're a pragmatic person, Corporal Grayson."

"When you're in a war, reality is the name of the game. You're a cop. You must understand that," he said gruffly, then regretted his harsh tone. He watched as she carefully spooned up a mouthful of eggs and started chewing. The look on her face was one of pure pleasure. She closed her eyes.

"Mmm…I never thought eggs could taste so good…."

If someone felt guilty right now, it was Quinn. The hollowness in Kerry's cheeks told him more than he wanted to know.

"How long, really, since you ate last?"

Sighing, Kerry opened her eyes. "Probably twenty-four hours or more."

Quinn reached down and pulled out a canteen filled with water.

"Here. You're probably thirsty, too."

As she took the dark green canteen, her fingers met his briefly. Kerry absorbed his touch. The look in his eyes was predatory and assessing. "You don't miss much, do you?" There was a wry note in her voice as she set the MRE aside, unscrewed the lid of the canteen and drank deeply of the proffered gift of water.

After a moment, Kerry forced herself to stop drinking. She had to think of others, too. Reluctantly, she put down the canteen, wiped her mouth with the back of her hand and then started to replace the cap.

"You're not finished."

"Yes, I am."

"No, you're not. Drink up." Quinn hooked a thumb toward his pack. "I've got a gallon of water in there. More than enough for the three of us."

Kerry hesitated. She remembered once more those who were thirsty outside her hovel. She had heard too many squalls of infants dying of thirst. Seen too many desperate parents looking for water for their children. Her fingers tightened around the canteen, which rested on her knee.

When Kerry hung her head, her knuckles white as she gripped the canteen, understanding hit Quinn like a steamroller. Frowning, he lowered his voice.

"Listen to me, Kerry. I was in the Gulf War. I was over there in the worst of it. I saw a lot of people die of thirst—men, women and children. It wasn't fair. And it wasn't right. But the first thing you have to do is take care of yourself. You're the only one here who has the information we need. You can't short yourself just because people out there need water, too. Without you, this whole operation in Area Five would fall apart. I need you strong. Thinking. Not weak and unable to put two thoughts together.''

His voice was gentle with understanding. Kerry lifted her head and drowned in his lambent blue gaze, which was fraught with emotion. Slowly, she picked up the canteen again. Taking off the top, she lifted it to her lips and drank deeply. For the first time in two weeks, she was able to drink all the water she really wanted. What a luxury!

Wiping her mouth, she gave him a sad look. ''I still feel guilty.''

''That's okay,'' Quinn rumbled. ''Life isn't fair. It isn't ever gonna be. You've earned the right to the water, and—'' he gestured toward the half-eaten MRE ''—the rest of this food.''

Grimacing, Kerry handed the canteen back to him. ''Thanks,'' she whispered.

''Eat.''

''I can't....''

''Why not?''

Rubbing her stomach, she gave him a helpless look. ''I've been so long without good food that if I ate that, I'd throw up, Corporal. I'd be better off eating a crust of bread, or some crackers....''

Wincing internally, Quinn said nothing. He pulled one of the lunch MREs toward him, tore it open and took out a handful of crackers. ''Here, start with these. We'll slowly build you up in the next day or two so you *can* eat regular food.''

Kerry took the crackers and peeled off the plastic with shaky fingers. Her stomach growled, embarrassingly loud.

''I guess my belly knows it's going to get fed.''

Moodily, Quinn watched as she daintily ate each cracker as if it were a priceless gift. A look of pleasure suffused her face once again as she tasted the morsels. It hurt to watch her. This was America, the richest nation on earth, and people were starving to death. The terrible reality of that slammed into him. Kerry Chelton was gaunt looking. So was Petula. And so were the men who had taken the bottled water off the Huey earlier. Everyone had obviously dropped weight. Alarmingly so. As Quinn sat there listening to Petula breathing softly in her sleep, cuddling her purple dinosaur, and watching Kerry eat each cracker as if it were a feast, rage rose in him.

It was a rage of frustration. Flying in, he'd seen how every road in the basin, large and small, had been ripped up and torn apart by the massive earthquake. No vehicle, no convoy could possibly get through to give the people a consistent supply line of food. Now, as he sat here with Kerry and the little girl, the human side of the disaster was brought home to him in a way he'd never thought he'd see in the United States.

''You know,'' he said, his voice rough with sudden feeling, "things like this happen overseas. You see it on television. You see the destruction. Yeah, you feel bad, but it doesn't reach you or grab your heart and gut." Looking around the hut she'd fashioned as a strong wind blew in through the many cracks in the walls, he said, "But now it's happening here. In America. Our home." With a shake of his head, he held her darkened eyes. "God, it's just sinking in…this disaster…."

Without thinking, Kerry reached out, her hand covering his momentarily. "It's a nightmare. And it's unraveling by the minute, Corporal Grayson." Her gesture had been an attempt to try and soothe his obvious shock over the conditions around him. But once she realized what she was doing, Kerry jerked her hand away. Heat stung her neck and flowed up into her face. What on earth was she thinking, touching him like that? Glancing up, she saw his blue eyes suddenly become stormy. What *was* that emotion she saw for a split second on his hardened features?

Unsure, Kerry said, "Don't mind me. I'm a toucher. I found out a long time ago that people respond better if you reach out and just touch them. Stabilize them. It sends a message, a good one."

Nodding, he rasped, "I'm reeling, all right. I won't tell my men that. I'm sure they're just as shell-shocked by what they're seeing right now as I am." His hand tingled pleasantly where her fingertips had grazed his hairy flesh. Her touch was unexpected. Wonderful. He wanted more. Much more.

"When we're alone, call me Quinn. Out there—" he nodded toward the blanketed door "—call me Corporal Grayson. And I'll call you Deputy Chelton."

"Agreed." She saw his face thaw a bit. Maybe Grayson wasn't the unfeeling military machine that he'd projected earlier. He certainly looked like it, but Kerry knew that in law enforcement as well as the military, one had to hide behind an armored facade, show no emotion, and get the job done no matter what.

"Call me Kerry. Formality is necessary sometimes, but not always. We're a team. I'd like to think of you and your men as friends come to help us."

Friends. Well, Quinn wanted to say *Friends, hell. I'd like to be your lover.* Having no idea where all these crazy, intrusive thoughts and feelings were coming from, he quirked his mouth.

"Yeah, we're one big family in a hurt locker."

Laughing softly, Kerry said, "Spoken like a marine." "Hurt locker" was a navy slang term for someone being in a world of trouble. Since the Marine Corps was part of the navy, and because she had worked with military personnel in the past on a number of investigations, Kerry was familiar with the terminology. She saw Quinn's eyes shine with laughter for just a moment.

"And I have a feeling you're just one big softy underneath that tough marine-green facade of yours," she teased gently.

"Humph. We'll see."

Kerry motioned to the sleeping child. "She touched you. You knew she was hungry. The first thing you did, Quinn, was try to help her. And me." Her throat closed up for a moment. Bowing her head, Kerry felt tears jamming into her eyes. Unable to look at him, because she didn't want him to see the tears, she got to her feet and turned away. If she didn't, she was going to burst into tears—tears she'd fought off since the night of the quake. And right now wasn't the time or place to let them flow.

Clearing her throat, she whispered in a rough tone, "Come on. I'll get one of the women to stay with Petula. I need to show you how things are working around here."

Chapter Three

January 14: 0950

Sylvia Espinoza, a teenager of nineteen, came to stay with Petula so that Kerry could begin to show Quinn the layout of the area. The sun was shining strong and bright in the eastern sky when Quinn and she left her makeshift home. The day was chilly, and Kerry shrugged into her dark green jacket. As always, she wore her pistol around her waist and kept her flak jacket on beneath her blouse. With Diablo roving around, Kerry didn't want to take any chances.

As she fell into step beside Quinn, she felt more relief sheeting through her.

"I feel like we're going to make it now," she

confided to him. Around them, the world was waking up. People slept out in the open on cardboard, with whatever blankets they could find. To sleep in one of the remaining buildings would be foolhardy, given the continuing aftershocks. A roof or wall caving in could kill them.

Quinn glanced at Kerry's profile, which was set and serious. Her brows were drawn downward, her lips pursed. She had wrapped her arms across her chest, her hands beneath her armpits to keep them warm. January mornings in California were typically cold. Quinn made another mental note to call in for warm clothing for him and his men—and her.

"What do you mean?" Looking ahead, he saw that they were skirting the shopping area and heading toward the distribution center. In the distance, he saw one of his marines standing at ease, M-16 in place, as a long line of people waited patiently to receive bottled water.

Giving a short laugh, Kerry said, "Oh, I know this is going to sound stupid. Naive, really. I'm a police officer. I know better." She held his sharp blue gaze and her smile faded. "But just having you and your team here makes me feel better."

"In what way?" Quinn hoped she wasn't expecting miracles they couldn't deliver. There was just too much devastation and not enough people power to rescue even those most affected.

"Oh," Kerry murmured, "for two weeks I've shouldered all the responsibility of trying to set up a logistical network to help people. I did receive training in disaster relief for our county, and it sure has come in handy. Without it, I wouldn't have had a *clue* what to do first.''

''You've handled this area single-handedly?''

''Yes.'' With a sigh, Kerry whispered, ''When the quake hit I had just gone out to my cruiser in the parking lot at the back of the sheriff's building, Quinn. I remember hearing this god-awful roar— like a freight train bearing down on me. I looked around, but it was dark and I couldn't see a thing. I didn't figure out what was happening until the first shock hit.''

Quinn slowed his pace and stopped, turning to face her. The emotions and pain in her expression ate at him as she stopped before him, looked down and began gnawing on her lower lip, obviously struggling not to cry. Without thinking, he reached out and slid his hand down her arm.

''It's okay,'' he murmured. As a trained EMT, he knew the effect touch and a gentle voice could have on someone who was in trauma. It was obvious to him that Kerry was still in shock. Deep shock. She refused to look up at him. He wanted to touch her again, so he rested his hand lightly on her slumped shoulder and stepped toward her until their bodies were nearly touching. What she needed, he realized, was to talk it out, to get some of those nightmarish memories out of her in the same way a sick person needed to discharge an infection in order to feel better.

"Tell me about it?"

The deep, concerned tone of Quinn's voice tore away the last of Kerry's defenses against the horror she could still see, even with her eyes tightly shut. His hand resting on her shoulder sent warm, wonderful sensations lapping through her. His attention, his obvious care, dismantled her monumental efforts to put a lid on the boiling cauldron of trauma she carried daily within her.

"I don't know if you're ready to hear it," she said unsteadily.

Quinn patted her shoulder awkwardly. Hell, if he was honest with himself, he really wanted to open his arms and draw Kerry against him. That's what she needed most. With all the people around them, however, Quinn knew that wasn't wise. She was a leader and needed to be seen that way by the people of the area. And he didn't want his stature as head of the fire team to be compromised, either. So he remained where he was, even though his heart was crying to him to embrace Kerry. Hold her, rock her and ease the awful pain he saw revealed in her pale features.

Biting down hard on her lower lip, Kerry tried to control her escaping emotions. "Oh, this isn't going to be good, Quinn. I don't think you want a crybaby on your hands right now...."

Chuckling softly, he said, "Listen, Kerry, I've

seen horror. I know trauma. I think I've got an idea
of what you're going through. One thing I found out
a long time ago was that it helps to talk it out with
someone you trust. Someone you feel safe with.''

Lifting her chin, Kerry tried to smile, but failed.
''You make me feel safe, Quinn. I can't explain it.
The moment I saw you come off that Huey, I knew
everything was going to be okay. Maybe that's fool-
ish and idealistic, but that's how you impressed
me.'' Easing her hands from beneath her armpits she
waved them helplessly, her voice wobbling as she
said, ''The sheriff's building collapsed in on itself,
Quinn. All three stories.'' Kerry shut her eyes. Hot
tears scalded her eyelids. She felt his hand grip her
shoulder more tightly, as if to buttress her against
the pain she was sharing with him.

''Go on...'' Damn, it was tough just to stand here
and not hold her. Quinn watched as two tears wound
down her pale cheeks, leaving a silvery path in the
light film of dust on her skin. How badly he wanted
to give Kerry a warm, luxurious bath, so she could
relax. She needed to clean herself up to feel halfway
human again. He was glad she'd said he made her
feel safe. His heart had soared at that whispered admission, and emotion still vibrated in his chest, like
a flower that had discovered the glory of the sun.
She made him feel good about himself as a man.

Sniffing, Kerry wiped her eyes self-consciously.
Raising her head, she looked around, worried that
others might see her crying. In the two weeks since

the disaster, she hadn't shed any tears. People were looking to her for strength, for answers and for organization. They looked to her for help. It was a horrible burden to carry alone.

"This is tougher to talk about than I thought," she admitted, taking a short rasping breath.

"I'm here for you, Kerry. Just talk it out. That's best." And it was. To get a victim of trauma to talk was part of the healing process.

"Well..." She looked up at him and was stunned to see the tender flame burning in his blue eyes. That hard, armored marine mask had dissolved. The man who stood in front of her now took her breath away. His well-shaped mouth had softened, his lips slightly parted. The gentle strength she saw in his face made him even more handsome.

"I'm listening,...."

"The building collapsed, Quinn. I was thrown off my feet and rolled around in the parking lot. The cruiser I was going to climb into flipped. I was lucky I wasn't crushed. I remember seeing the back end of the car suddenly shooting upward. The streetlights went off. Everything went black. So black... The roar around me was incredible. I've never heard anything like it before. I remember getting thrown against the cyclone wire fence—smashing into it. I heard the building going down. Dust...dust was everywhere. I was choking on it. I couldn't see. I was covered with it. I don't know how long the shock lasted...."

"The initial quake lasted two minutes."

"It felt like *hours,*" Kerry whispered unsteadily. She blinked back the tears, mesmerized by his tender expression. How badly she wanted to take one more step toward him and sink into his arms. Somehow, Kerry knew that Quinn Grayson would hold her. Hold her, help her and heal her. Right now, her heart was wide-open and she was feeling so many emotions for the first time since the quake. It was him, she realized belatedly—his care, his attention, the touch of his hand resting gently on her shoulder, that had allowed her this moment of healing.

"Hours..." she repeated, and slowly shook her head.

"Then what happened?" Quinn asked, trying to keep his voice steady. He saw the ravages of horror in Kerry's wide, tear-filled eyes. Her mouth was a slash against the awful feelings she held within her, and it hurt him to see her suffering. How much he wanted to take his thumbs and erase the tracks of those tears. But Quinn knew the value of letting a person cry. When he'd worked as an EMT, they'd had an old expression: better out than in. In other words, it was better to cry, scream or talk about the incident rather than hold it inside. If a victim tried to suppress the hurt, it became like an ugly infection that would debilitate the person sooner or later.

"The building collapsed," Kerry said, all the energy draining out of her as she stood with that cold

January sunshine against her back. "Do you know how many people died in there, Quinn?"

He shook his head, seeing the grief now shadowing her face. "No...no, I don't, Kerry."

"I—I had so many friends in there, men and women I'd worked with for years.... Since Lee got killed, they'd rallied around me, helped me so much through that hellish year after I lost him...." She stopped and sniffed. Embarrassed, she raised her hand and tried to wipe away the tears. It was impossible. They were leaking out of her eyes steadily now. She felt as if a huge volcano of grief was imploding in her chest. A lump was forming in her throat, keeping her from saying anymore at the moment.

"Lee?" Quinn asked, stymied.

"My husband. He was a sheriff's deputy, too...." Kerry took a ragged breath. "I was married to Lee for three years. H-he was killed in the line of duty. He didn't like to wear his flak jacket under his shirt, so he rarely did. He got a call one night on duty, and when he went to the scene, a gang member shot him point-blank in the chest. If he'd had his vest on, it would have saved his life. But he didn't...."

"Damn," Quinn whispered, his fingers digging momentarily into her shoulder. "I'm sorry, Kerry. Really sorry." And he was. It was obvious she loved her husband. Quinn could see the warmth burning in her tearful gray eyes when she spoke of him.

Wouldn't it be wonderful if some woman loved him that way? Yes, but it was never going to happen.

Pushing aside his own problems, Quinn focused on Kerry. She lifted her hands and wiped her face. All the gesture did was spread the dust, leaving muddy smears. Withdrawing his own hand, he groped for the canteen and a cloth he carried in one of the pockets of his uniform.

"Did you lose all your friends in there?" he asked, as he uncapped the canteen and poured some of the precious water onto the dark green cloth in his hand.

"Y-yes. Every one of them. We had a shift change going on at the time. After the first shock ended, I got to my feet. I was stunned. It was so dark. There were no lights. The quake had torn up the lighting system and it was awful. I managed to find my flashlight and started back toward what I thought was a building." Opening her hands, she looked down at them. Her nails were jagged, and her hands were dirty and covered with cuts.

"I tripped and fell so many times in that chewed-up asphalt parking lot, Quinn. It was pulverized rubble, just like you see here at the shopping center." She swept her arm around them. The once smooth surface was now a vast stretch of jagged chunks of asphalt and dirt that looked more like a plowed field than a parking lot.

"But you got to the building?" Quinn capped the canteen and hung it back on his web belt.

Kerry nodded and sighed heavily. "Yes, I managed to get over to it. But I could smell natural gas. The lines had been broken. I knew I was in trouble. As I got closer to the building, I couldn't believe it. All three stories had pancaked down upon one another. Three stories had become a half story of concrete, steel and glass rubble." Shaking her head, she whispered, "All I could do was stand there. I just couldn't believe it. I didn't hear anyone crying out for help. Nothing. I felt so helpless. So very helpless. I stumbled and staggered all around that building, but there was nothing left of it. Over a hundred people were in that structure...so many of them my friends...." She covered her face with her hands.

How alone she was, Quinn realized, her grief reaching out and grabbing him hard. *To hell with it,* he thought, stepping closer and putting his arm around her shoulders. "Come here, Kerry. Let me clean you up a bit." And he raised the dampened towel.

When she lifted her head in surprise, he smiled at her. It was a smile, he hoped, that said *Relax, I'm going to help you.*

With the first stroke of the soft terry cloth against her cheek, Kerry released a tremulous sigh. She stood very still against him while he cleaned her face as if she were a lost child in need of care and love. Every stroke was gentle. The coolness of the cloth against her skin felt good. Cleansing. Quinn was so close, and so pulverizingly male to Kerry. It took everything she had left, emotionally, not to turn and lay her head against his strong, broad shoulder. Somehow, Kerry knew Quinn could handle big loads and heavy responsibility. He was built for it not only physically, but emotionally, too.

His gentleness was surprising and unexpected, however. All too soon, he was done cleaning her face. Stepping away, he dropped his arm from her shoulders. Inwardly, Kerry cried over the loss of his nearness, his care. Opening her eyes, she fell captive to the smoky blueness now banked in his eyes as he studied her in silence. For the first time in years, Kerry felt another stirring deep within her heart and lower body—the start of desire for a man. For Quinn Grayson. Even though he was a tough, no-nonsense marine warrior, he had an incredibly surprising and wonderfully tender side to him, too. It was a beautiful discovery for Kerry. Right now, after the last two hellish weeks, she needed someone exactly like Quinn.

"Has anyone ever told you that you're really a mother hen in disguise?" Kerry tried to keep her voice light and teasing, for if she didn't, she was going to break down in unrelenting, body-shaking sobs. She hadn't yet cried for the loss of all her friends, and the emotions threatened to hit her hard now.

Grinning crookedly, Quinn handed her the damp towel. "Yeah, I've been accused of that by my fire team from time to time. It's my job to care for my people.''

"You're good at it," Kerry whispered shakily. She took the towel and rubbed her hands free of dirt. "And this is a wonderful gift…. Thanks for listening to me, Quinn. And thanks for the spit bath. I know I'm dirty as all get-out. There's no water to waste. But I long so badly for a hot bath…." She sighed. "Now, *that's* a dream. A faraway one…"

Quinn said nothing, watching as she scrubbed her slender wrists and artistic fingers free of dirt. Once they were clean, he saw many fine pink scars across them, as well as healing cuts. "What are these from?" he asked, pointing to her hand.

"Those? Oh, I spent hours at the building trying to pull away rubble and debris to find someone…anyone…." Kerry handed the cloth back to him. When his fingers met hers, she absorbed the warmth like a greedy beggar. Right now, she felt like an emotional thief on the prowl, stealing energy from Quinn, who was giving so unselfishly to her. That wasn't right, but Kerry couldn't help herself. Quinn seemed to bring out every emotion she hadn't allowed herself to feel for the last two weeks. That caught Kerry off guard, and she labored beneath the violent ebb and flow of her grief, rage, frustration and sadness.

"Any luck?" he asked, tucking the cloth back into the large pocket in the thigh of his cammos.

Shaking her head, Kerry felt sadness overwhelm

her once more. "No...none. Not one survived. I stayed there all the next day, Quinn, but I couldn't find anyone alive, or hear any cries for help. It was just so...devastating."

Looking around the shopping center, Quinn could see people moving about. Here and there, he saw small campfires, with people huddled around them for warmth. They were cooking a meager breakfast. Probably preparing whatever food they could find.

"The natural gas odor got so bad, I had to leave. I was afraid of an explosion," Kerry related.

"We heard at the base that there were a lot of explosions and fires after the quake."

Nodding, Kerry said, "Yes, there were. There aren't now. The pipelines have all been shut off."

"So how did you get involved in all of this?" He swept his arm around the area.

"By accident, I guess." Kerry shrugged. "I retrieved what I could out of my cruiser—the shotgun, the emergency medical kit, my shoulder radio—and went looking for a place where I might find some electricity, a generator. Uppermost in my mind was to get help. There was a hardware store two blocks down from the sheriff's building and across the street from the apartment where I used to live. I went there and dug out a small gasoline generator. About five blocks down, there was a small electronics store. I broke into what was left of it and found a radio that hadn't been destroyed. The gas station was still standing for some reason, and I managed to siphon off gas from a car that was nearby. I carried the container of gas to the generator, and got it fired up and working. Once it was on-line, I hooked up the radio and started calling for help. By chance, I got lucky and zeroed in on Logistics at Camp Reed. From there, I talked to Morgan Trayhern, who, thankfully, was able to get you here. You and the supplies." Kerry grimaced. "I needed a place for a helicopter to land, so I set off to try and find a big enough clearing. The shopping center was a mile away, so I came here. The asphalt parking lot was chewed up, but the area was clear of downed power lines and there was no natural gas or propane around. I told Morgan about it, and that's when he started ordering the Huey to fly in as often as it could during the daylight hours to deliver food, water and medicine."

"And so you set up your H.Q. here as a result?"

"Yes." Kerry smiled softly. "I asked for volunteers to help me move the generator and radio to this place. The people who lived in this area pitched in with their hearts and souls. They're wonderful, Quinn. Most of them have lost family members. But they rallied and helped me. Over the last two weeks, this neighborhood has really pulled together in order to survive. These people are great. The area has a mix of nationalities—lots of Koreans, Hispanics. Elderly folks on a fixed income… It's a poor area of Los Angeles. But everyone—" she glanced over at him "—and I mean *everyone,* has helped. They understand that the only way they're going to survive this is to work together as a team.''

''So there's been no fighting among them for food or water?''

''None. They're a tribute to the human race, Quinn.'' Kerry wrinkled her nose. ''But then, a week ago, Diablo started infiltrating, and it has been hell ever since. We aren't prepared for such a group—men who take and don't share. There aren't any guns available to fight them off, either—the houses are crushed. You can't dig inside to find anything, not with aftershocks happening dozens of times a day.'' Touching her holster at her side, she added, ''I'm the only one with a weapon. But I can't be everywhere. If I go somewhere, I have to walk. I can't just hop in my cruiser, lights flashing, and go to the scene where I'm needed.''

''I understand,'' Quinn said. His admiration for Kerry skyrocketed. She was an incredibly resourceful woman. Single-handedly, this stalwart person was helping hundreds of people survive. And as Quinn looked around, watching quake survivors get up from their shabby, crude sleep areas, he began to understand that Kerry was a very special person. Her bravery, her strength under the circumstances, was worthy of a medal. Her cool-headed efforts, her ability to organize and be a leader when the world was in chaos around her, spoke volumes.

''Let's get to your distribution center,'' he told her with a slight, tender smile. ''Let's see what we

can do to help you and these folks out a little more.''
He knew his first priority was to close down the bad
guys if possible, but even now, he could see his
mission changing, just as Morgan had warned that
it might.

Hope spiraled strongly in her breast. As Quinn
gazed at her, Kerry felt her heart expanding with
such joy that it overshadowed all the sadness she
was feeling. There was a burning look in his eyes
meant for her alone, and she knew it. Somehow, her
sharing the awful trauma with Quinn had forged a
new and wonderful connection between them. Kerry
was as scared as she was euphoric. Never had she
felt like this. As she walked at Quinn's side once
more, she told herself it was because she was traumatized, her emotions stripped and vulnerable.
Quinn represented help and survival, she tried to tell
herself sternly. And that was all. But no matter what
she did, she couldn't quite make herself believe that
completely. No, there was another emotion, a special
one, growing between them. She had seen it banked
in his narrowed eyes…and she was afraid of it.
Afraid, and yet eager at the very same time.

Chapter Four

January 14: 1015

Private Orvil Perkins gave Quinn a look that spoke volumes. The thin, wiry marine was surrounded by civilians who had desperate looks on their faces and in their eyes as they asked him question after question. As Kerry and Quinn approached, the crowd of about twenty people, mostly adults, turned to face them, hope burning in their eyes.

In shock, Quinn saw that the people were all dirty and unkempt. It looked as if he'd stepped into a third world country. He'd been in some, but he'd never seen people in such a state. Even in those countries, people were able to bathe, wash their threadbare clothes and keep their hair neat and combed. Not here. These people were gaunt, with red-rimmed eyes, their hands caked with dirt. The desperation in their faces rocked him deeply.

"Is help coming?" One balding man spoke up, his voice booming across the others.

"My baby," a woman cried. "She's got a fever and I can't get it down. I can't even get to the aspirin in our house. It's too dangerous to crawl in and try to find it. Can you help me?"

"We need water," another man said. "We aren't getting enough. My animals have already died. I've got a teenage son with a broken leg. I can't move him. I need more water for him. Can you help us?"

Swallowing hard, Quinn placed his rifle across his right shoulder. Holding up his hand, he silenced the restless, anxious group.

"My name is Corporal Grayson. The Marine Corps is beginning to initiate help. You are in Area Five, as most of you probably already know. We're here to provide safety as well as continuing organization."

"When are we going to get medical help?" a red-haired woman called out angrily. "I got a little girl, six years old, and she's diabetic! I gotta have insulin or—" she choked up "—she's gonna die! You gotta help me!"

Kerry lifted her hands to silence them. "Folks, I know your stories and your needs. Today, Corporal Grayson is going to assign one of his men to write down each of your specific requests. We'll pass them along to the Huey crew that flies in our supplies. That's the best we can do. There're millions of people in the basin just as bad off, or worse, than us. Corporal Grayson is the beginning of a vanguard, but he can't do everything. He and his fire team are here primarily to protect us from Diablo.''

A sigh of relief went up from the crowd, which edged closer and closer. Kerry saw Quinn cut her a quick glance. He said nothing to her about her suggestion. They hadn't talked about it, but Kerry knew it would help defuse the anxiety if written requests were collected.

''Thank God!'' a man cried. ''Those bastards killed my wife!'' He began to sob, and pressed his hands against his face. ''All for a lousy box of crackers.''

Quinn stared at the man, who appeared in his thirties. He was weeping uncontrollably.

Kerry gripped Quinn's left arm. ''Folks, please get back into line for your water ration. I need to take Corporal Grayson around our immediate area, fill him in on our needs, so he can radio back to Logistics at Camp Reed. It's there that plans for the future are worked out. The more information I can give the corporal, the more potential help we can get.''

''We need medicine! I need insulin!'' the woman cried, desperation in her tone. ''My baby's gonna die without it! Somebody has to do *something* soon!"

"I hear you," Kerry said soothingly. "And help is coming. Just get into line, Martha. Please."

The crowd began to hesitantly break up. People trudged wearily back into a ragged line to await the one-quart bottle of water that would have to suffice for them and their families for the next twenty-four hours.

Quinn felt Kerry release his arm and he glanced at her. The look in her soft gray eyes compounded the emotions he felt in his chest. As they moved out of earshot, he growled, "I never realized how bad off these people really were. Not until now..."

Mouth compressed, Kerry nodded. "You've seen only the tip of the iceberg, Quinn." Her voice broke with emotion as she added, "Believe me."

He halted and turned to face her. "You've been holding this paper bag on wheels around here together since the beginning, haven't you?"

"Yes." Shrugging, she sent the people waiting in line a compassionate look. "I'm a law enforcement officer. It's my duty to help keep the peace. To help direct people in a disaster."

"You're doing a helluva lot more than that." Giving the crowd a dark look, he returned his gaze to Kerry. "I like your idea of having them write down their needs. That woman has to have insulin for her daughter. We need them to write this stuff down, and then we can go through it like a triage, separating common requests from real emergencies. Thanks for suggesting it.''

Smiling slightly, Kerry said, ''I didn't mean to usurp your authority. It was one of the things I thought of doing once you guys arrived.''

''It's a good suggestion. Speak up on anything else you have in mind. Frankly, I wasn't trained for this kind of duty.''

''Who was?'' Kerry asked wryly, giving him a tentative half smile. She liked the way his blue eyes warmed when he looked at her. Despite Quinn's warrior toughness, he was a man with a heart. A big, generous heart.

''I read you loud and clear on that one. Let's make a circuit around the shopping center. From the looks of it, a lot of people are sleeping out in the parking lot, with makeshift tents, and cardboard for beds. I want to see the whole thing. Then we'll go back to your H.Q. and make plans. I also want to radio Logistics and try to get an extra flight out here today with certain supplies that you think are needed right away.''

''The insulin, for sure,'' Kerry said.

''Absolutely…''

As Quinn turned and began to walk again, with Kerry at his side, he wrestled with the exploding shock of seeing Americans in such a state of help-lessness. He felt overwhelmed by it all. They were only a five-man marine fire team. His main mission was to hunt down Diablo, but how was he going to do that and try to help these people, too? Torn, Quinn knew that Kerry's help, as well the knowledge she'd gained from the past two weeks of dealing with this horrific situation, was absolutely essential to him in order to make good decisions for everyone here. And he knew Morgan would support his helping the people first, before trying to locate Diablo. One fire team could do only so much.

January 14: 1515

By 1500, Quinn had radioed in for some extra supplies—emergency items needed to keep people alive. Luckily, according to Morgan Trayhern, Camp Reed had just gotten ten more helicopters delivered, U.S. Navy choppers that would hold a lot more cargo. They were setting up a dirt landing zone at Camp Reed, a second, makeshift airport desperately needed in this escalating situation. Marines at Camp Reed were now moving supplies to this new airport so that the larger, heavier helicopters could carry more supplies in one flight to each affected area.

Kerry had looked tired as Quinn had stood outside her hovel and made the radio call. Sylvia was babysitting Petula nearby.

Quinn had shared more of his MREs with them, but Sylvia had gobbled her food down and promptly thrown up. The food was too rich for her in her starving condition. She'd cried afterward because she hadn't listened to Kerry's instructions to eat just a little, slowly, and then eat more an hour later. The teenage girl was so hungry she'd eaten like a starving dog. Quinn had felt badly for her. He'd seen the unshed tears in Kerry's eyes as she'd held the girl while she vomited. This was an unfolding and shocking nightmare to him. And it was going to get worse.

In his eyes, the only good thing about the situation was Kerry. She was a bulwark of quiet, gentle strength. Throughout the day, her home was like headquarters for the area. Anyone who needed something came to Kerry. By late afternoon, she had given away the two extra blankets she slept on to two needy families who had nothing and were sleeping out on the yellowed lawns outside their destroyed homes, huddled together to keep warm. The only blanket she didn't give away was Petula's and the ones that hung in the door of their hovel.

Once Sylvia was feeling better she took Petula for a walk, and Quinn took the opportunity to sit with Kerry outside her home. She looked drawn.

The sun was low in the sky, on the opposite side of the shopping center now, leaving the house in the shade. Kerry was sitting on the chewed-up ground sifting through at least fifty handwritten notes before her. Her brows were drawn downward, but as the breeze lifted some of the strands of her hair, she looked beautiful to him.

Opening the pack he left inside the hovel, Quinn knelt down opposite her and prepared a heating tab.

Kerry looked over. "What are you doing?" Quinn had two tin cups in hand and several packets near his boot.

"Making us some well-deserved instant coffee." He grinned at her. "Interested?" He tore open the pack and sprinkled it into the bottom of a cup, then added water.

Sighing, Kerry whispered, "Coffee?"

The longing in her voice touched him. "Yeah. Not the real stuff, and certainly not a mocha latte, but it'll do in a pinch, as my ma would say. Want some?" The moment he lifted his head, he drowned in her widening eyes. When they were alone, Quinn noticed, Kerry's official demeanor melted away. He was privileged to see the real woman behind the badge. And he liked what he saw—more than he should. All day he'd found reasons to touch her arm or hand or shoulder briefly. Quinn *liked* touching Kerry. Every time he did, he saw her expression change perceptibly. Saw her dove-gray eyes go soft for just a moment. And it made his heart sing. He felt his chest expanding and widening like a river flowing at flood stage. Kerry Chelton was affecting him like no other woman he'd ever met. And Quinn found himself dying to know all about her on a personal level.

Yet all day they'd dealt with people, with problems, trying to come up with solutions to help them. It was a pathetically useless effort, as far as Quinn was concerned. They didn't have medicine, blankets, food or water for the people, except what was being flown in hourly, and that merely helped stave off the long-term problems.

"Coffee…" Kerry sighed. "Wow! Do you know, in my dream last night, I was at a Starbucks over on Central?" She hooked her thumb over her shoulder. "Just two blocks from where I worked there was a Starbucks. Now it's gone. I used to love to get my coffee there before I went on shift."

Chuckling, Quinn created a tiny stove with some pieces of asphalt and placed the cup between them. The magnesium tab flared to life, bright and burning. Soon, the water was bubbling. "Yeah, I don't move without my coffee, so I know what you mean."

Smiling, Kerry placed her hands over the papers so they wouldn't blow away in the breeze. The sky was a light blue, the sun bright. She looked forward to the afternoons because the temperature warmed up and she could take off her coat. By this time of day, the chill and dampness of the night before was only a memory.

"You have the most wonderful soft, Southern accent, Quinn. Were you born in the South?'' she asked as he lifted one cup off and set it aside, then placed the second one over the burning tab. She saw his cheeks grow a dull red as she complimented him. Even though he'd shaved that morning, a five-o'clock shadow darkened his face, giving him a dangerous, predatory look. It excited her.

''I was born in Kentucky. Up in the mountains. My folks are hill people.'' Quinn held up sugar and cream. ''Any of these?''

''Oh, yes, please. One of each?''

The sudden excitement in her voice made him sad. Kerry's eyes were bright with eagerness for such a small, seemingly insignificant gift. After he tore each packet open and poured the contents into the steaming coffee, he stirred it with a spoon. ''There,'' he murmured, and held the cup toward her. ''Coffee for a purty lady.''

Blushing, Kerry laughed. It was the first time in weeks that she had. Her hand closed around the handle of the cup. ''Thanks, Quinn. You are truly an angel in Marine Corps disguise.''

''Drink up,'' he told her brusquely, unable to meet the gentle look of thanks in her eyes. ''You've more than earned this cup of coffee.'' And she had. Quinn was finding that Kerry was giving away everything she had to those who were worse off than she.

As the second cup came to a boil, Quinn removed

it and took a sip. He liked his coffee black and strong. Over the rim, he saw the look of absolute pleasure on Kerry's face as she drank.

"Ohh... I never knew coffee could taste so good, Quinn. This is delicious...." She closed her eyes and savored the taste of it.

His conscience ate at him. Back at Camp Reed, they had real coffee in huge urns, available twenty-four hours a day at the many chow tents that had been hastily erected in different parts of the hundred-thousand-acre military base. Dipping his head, he sipped his coffee with a scowl. The soft sighs of pleasure emanating from Kerry as she relished each sip ripped at his heart. She deserved so much more. She was a good person in a very ugly situation—so brave and helpful to those in need. In his eyes, Kerry deserved a medal, but she'd never get one. After what he'd seen this afternoon, Quinn knew that just surviving in this area was heroic.

Opening her eyes, Kerry smiled at Quinn, who sat with a dark scowl on his face. He seemed bothered by something, but wasn't saying much.

"You said you were born in the mountains of Kentucky. Like the Hatfields and McCoys?" she teased, trying to lighten his mood.

"Yeah, you could say that." Fighting the sadness and frustration he felt for the people around them, Quinn looked at Kerry. Just studying her attractive features and gray eyes lifted his spirits and made his heart pound a little harder for a moment.

"I was barefoot most of the time until I went to a local high school nearby. Up until then, I was home-schooled by my ma. My pa was a man of the woods. He hunted and killed what we needed for food. My ma tended a huge garden, and me and my sisters used to help her can stuff in the fall. When I wasn't book learnin', my pa would take me out and teach me how to hunt and track."

"What a wonderful childhood," Kerry said. "I was born and raised here in Ontario, California, a huge suburb of Los Angeles. I'm afraid I'm a city girl in comparison to you."

"Opposites."

"What made you join the Marine Corps?" she asked, sipping the cooling coffee with relish.

"My pa was in the corps. So were my uncles, and my granddaddy before them. It's a tradition in our family."

"Are you making it a career?"

"Probably." Quinn shrugged. "I don't know anything else. I'm not a math wizard. I don't pretend to be smart like a college graduate."

"The fact that you didn't go to college doesn't mean you aren't intelligent," Kerry pointed out. "Look how many good ideas you've come up with so far. You're good at assessing a situation and coming up with solutions."

Feeling heat steal into his face, Quinn shrugged. "I'm fire team leader. It's my job to do that."

"I feel your common sense and practical knowledge are a huge plus here. You dovetail beautifully with me and my ideas."

"Yeah, we make a good team," he admitted quietly. Glancing around, he could see people getting ready for nightfall, which would happen around 1730 this time of year.

"I was so looking forward to your coming," Kerry admitted. "Today I realized just how tired I've become—mostly because I wasn't eating much." She gave a short laugh. "You can't get far on a growling stomach. It's been tough pushing myself through my physical tiredness to keep going."

"I don't know how you've done it." And he didn't. His admiration for Kerry came through loud and clear in his voice. "You're so patient with people."

"You have to be, Quinn. That was part of my training as a deputy."

"Yeah, but a lot of it is you. You're a good person, Kerry. Mighty good, as my ma would say."

She laughed softly. "Thanks, that means a lot to me, Quinn." She gestured toward him. "So tell me about yourself. Are you married to some woman who loves the outdoors as much as you? Is she in base housing on Camp Reed with you? And do you have kids? You'd be a great father, I think."

Startled by her personal questions, he was caught off guard. "I'm not married," he told her gruffly, "so there're no rug rats around."

Kerry grinned. "Rug rats? That's a military term for kids, right?"

"Yeah. A nice term."

She tilted her head. Kerry couldn't believe Quinn didn't have a woman in his life. She'd seen a shadow flicker in his blue eyes when she'd asked.

"Sorry," she whispered. "I guess I got nosy and overstepped my bounds with you. You just seemed like you were married and settled down. I could imagine you with a couple of kids—taking them fishing and hiking in the woods. Doing the kind of things that give children a wonderful sense of the natural world that surrounds them."

Quinn finished his coffee. "I was engaged once," he admitted abruptly. "But Frannie wasn't happy that I was a marine. She was a social climber, to be blunt about it. I was an enlisted man and I found out too late that she wanted someone with more rank and status. Like an officer."

Grimacing, Kerry sipped the last of her coffee. She handed the empty cup to Quinn. Their fingertips met briefly, and again she enjoyed the contact. His demeanor made her feel solid and secure. Protection emanated from Quinn like warmth and light from the sun. And she was starved for both.

"Sorry to hear that," Kerry murmured. "At least you found out before you tied the knot."

"Yeah," he muttered, putting the cups aside, "I did. She wasn't honest in our relationship, I discovered. And if I marry someday, which won't be soon, I want truth between us. My ma and pa have been married for over thirty years and I saw, growin' up, what it took to hold a marriage together. It's a lot of hard work, but I think it's worth the effort."

Resting her elbows on her crossed legs, Kerry smiled softly. "It sounds like what I had with Lee, my husband. And you're right, in the throwaway society we're in today, people waltz into marriage like it's a one-night gig at a local club, and waltz out of it the next day."

"It's far from that." Quinn glanced down at the watch on his right wrist. According to Morgan Trayhern, one of the big navy helos was going to try and come in just before dark to deliver an extra load of supplies, including the insulin that was so desperately needed. Quinn hadn't said anything to Kerry about it, because Trayhern couldn't promise it would arrive that quickly. But Morgan had told Quinn he'd go through hell and high water to try and get it off to him by the end of the day. This one shipment would make such a difference, and Quinn wanted nothing more than to give these people, including Kerry and little Petula, some respite from the horrible circumstances they dealt with daily.

"How did you meet your husband?" he asked now.

"We were at the police academy when we met." Kerry sighed. "Lee was a lot like you."

"Oh?"

"Yes, he was born and raised in the Sisque Mountains, in a tiny logging community in Northern California known as Happy Camp. His dad was a logger, his mother a teacher at the local school. Lee could hunt black bear and cougar when he was ten years old. His father taught him well."

"I see."

"I'm twenty-seven now. We got married after we graduated, when I was twenty-one." She lost her smile. "At least we had six wonderful years together. We worked for the same sheriff's department, though we had different areas to patrol. Our watch officer gave us the same hours so that we could at least have a life together outside work. We both had the graveyard shift."

"Any kids?" He didn't mean to ask that, but he suddenly had to know. So when he saw Kerry's face go pale and her gaze drop as she pretended to pick at a thread on her dusty, dark green slacks, he suddenly felt as if he'd tramped like a bull into the proverbial china shop. Obviously he'd touched on a very poignant subject, a raw wound in her life. "You don't have to answer that. Don't mind me. I shouldn't have asked," he told her abruptly.

"No..." Kerry said in a low tone, "I don't mind you asking, Quinn. I like talking with you, if you want to know the truth...." And she did. Forcing herself to look at him, Kerry saw the angst in his eyes. Opening her hands, she whispered, "I was pregnant with our first child when Lee got killed in the line of duty. When I heard from my watch chief that he was in the hospital, I went there. I remember fainting after the doctor came out and told me he was dead. Two other deputies were there and caught me. When I came to, a few minutes later, I had horrible cramping in my abdomen. I was numb with shock. They took me home and I remember just lying there on the couch, curled up, staring off into space. I couldn't believe it, Quinn...that Lee was dead."

"I'm sorry."

"There's more...." Kerry hitched up one shoulder in an awkward shrug. "I remember finally sleeping, probably near dawn. When I woke up, hours later, the cramping was worse. It was then that I miscarried. I was three months along and the shock of his death caused it." Biting her lower lip, she whispered, "So I lost our baby, too."

Quinn could hardly bear to look at her. He heard the sadness, the helplessness, in her voice, but there was nothing he could do to soothe her loss. Not a thing. And the good Lord knew, he wanted to. He wanted to do *something* to ease her agonizing burden.

Chapter Five

January 15: 0600

Quinn didn't have the heart to awaken Kerry at
dawn the next morning. He'd just finished his three
hours of duty at the distribution center, and had
come back to her hovel. Quietly easing away the
blanket over the door, he saw a scene that tugged at
his heart.

It has gotten very cold last night, with the wind
whipping and sawing inconstantly. Petula had left
her bed and made her way into Kerry's arms for
more warmth. Kerry lay on her side on the unfor-
giving cardboard beneath her, her legs drawn up toward her body. Curled in her arms, little Petula
snuggled, both of them sound asleep. Kerry had her
face pressed against Petula's hair.

Quinn stood there frozen, absorbing the heart-wrenching scene. It hurt him that all they had was cardboard to sleep on, now that Kerry had given the two Oriental rugs on the dirt floor to families who desperately needed something to cover up with during the cold nights. No one should live like this.

On top of everything else, he'd gotten a call that the navy helicopter wouldn't arrive until late today with the badly needed extra supplies. It had been held up because the medical items had to be flown in from San Francisco. Obliquely, he wondered if the little girl who needed insulin would survive until that afternoon. Frustration, he was discovering, was becoming his worst enemy.

Allowing the blanket over the door to fall into place because it kept out some of the biting wind, Quinn tried to be quiet as he moved about. Kerry had been up until 0100 this morning dealing with people who had problems, demands, urgent requests made worse by their rising hysteria. Word had gotten out that a marine team was here, and the news had run like wildfire across Area Five. When people heard that help had arrived, they came from miles around to the shopping center, pleading for relief.

After easing his rifle off his shoulder, Quinn slipped out of his Kevlar flak vest. He'd worn his heavy cammo jacket while standing on guard this morning because of the cold out there. When the night sky had begun to turn gray with the coming dawn, Private Cliff Ludlow had relieved him of guard duty. They had to keep an around-the-clock guard at the distribution center. Some people, beyond desperation, were sneaking in during the night to steal what little food or water might be left. Kerry couldn't stay up twenty-four hours a day to stand guard, so she couldn't stop the thievery until Quinn and his men had arrived to help.

When Private Ludlow had taken over, his eyes puffy from sleep, Quinn had purposely gone around the back of the shopping center, quietly moving among the massive piles of rubble, eyes open and ears keyed to any sounds. It had been silent, but Quinn didn't put it past Diablo to start trouble once they heard that a marine team had come in. Or the presence of the team might scare the gang away, possibly driving them into Area Six adjacent.

Now, as he quietly eased his hand into his massive pack and searched for three breakfast MREs, his mouth quirked in pain. Kerry had lost her baby due to the trauma of losing her husband. Trying to grasp how that must have felt, he shook his head. It was impossible to imagine. Taking the MREs from the pack, he quietly began to open them. More than anything, he'd like to waken them to a hot, decent breakfast. Little Petula had eaten off and on from the MRE he'd opened yesterday morning. According to Sylvia, the girl hadn't vomited once. By last night, Quinn could see the difference a little good food made for the girl. She was more animated, her wan cheeks touched with some color.

More than anything, he wanted Kerry to eat. He needed her strong and alert. She had the bad habit of giving away most of her food and supplies—even the rugs off her dirt floor—to those she saw as more needy than herself. What a big heart she had in that strong, beautiful body of hers.

Quinn quickly and efficiently fixed the three MREs, and when the enticing smells of eggs and bacon began filling the cold space within the hut, he glanced up.

Kerry was beginning to stir. Her eyes opened slightly, her lashes thick and dark against her pale flesh. The sight of the soft hair grazing her cheek made Quinn want to go over and gently tame the strands back into place, but he resisted. She slowly eased her left arm upward and rolled onto her back. Blinking, she raised her head.

He gave her a slight grin in greeting. "Breakfast is on, sweet pea."

Sweet pea. An endearment, Kerry realized vaguely as she struggled out of the deep folds of sleep that still tugged at her. Quinn sat near the door, his legs spread wide, the meals cooking on heating tabs before him. Light leaked in around the blanket at the door, leaving his hard face in shadow. The beard made him look truly like a warrior from the past. Maybe it was her sleep-fogged mind, Kerry thought as she gently extricated her arm from around Petula. Turning, she covered the child with both blankets, tucking them around Petula's bare feet.

Quinn said nothing as he savored the sight of Kerry wakening. Noticing the slight puffiness beneath her glorious, dark gray eyes, the softness of her full lips, he felt his heart mushroom violently with feelings for her. She sat up and rubbed her hands against her face.

"What time is it?" she asked, her voice husky with sleep.

"It's 0600—6:00 a.m. to you civilian types," he teased.

His voice was like rough sandpaper across her awakening senses, as delicious as a lover's caress. Lifting her head, she met his blue eyes, which were filled with warmth. Seeing the slight smile on his full mouth, she smiled shyly in return. He'd taken off his helmet, and his hair, dark and short, emphasized the shape of his large skull.

"That smells wonderful...." she whispered, moving slowly across the few feet of space to where he sat.

"Yes, and you're gonna eat *all* of your MRE today," he told her darkly, handing a plate along with some plastic utensils.

Thanking him softly, Kerry sat down nearby. She tucked her legs beneath her and balanced the warm plate on her right thigh. "Mmm...this is the best wake-up breakfast I've ever had! Thank you, Quinn. You're a knight in shining armor to me, to all of us...."

Watching her covertly, Quinn proceeded to wolf

down his own meal. So Kerry saw him as a knight...
His chest swelled with pride, and his heart hammered briefly. Tongue-tied, he didn't know how to reply to her husky words of thanks.

Kerry slowly ate the fluffy eggs, which were sprinkled with bits of diced red and green pepper and fragrant slices of onion. Her mouth watered as she spooned up the bacon. She knew she had to eat slowly and not gulp down the wonderful meal as she wanted to. No, she didn't want to follow Sylvia's example. Food was too precious to waste like that.

"We had five intruders last night," Quinn told her between bites. He stirred the hash browns with his plastic fork, his brow wrinkling for a moment. "Civilians, not Diablo."

"Desperate people."

Nodding, he rasped, "Yeah. It was pitiful. And every one of them had a sad story to tell, one that ripped my heart out. Some cried and begged me to give them just a bottle of water. Others had family members who are dying, who desperately need meds. I didn't realize how bad it really was out here, Kerry...."

Sadness flowed through her as she took another mouthful of eggs. "I know, Quinn. It's so tragic. It takes every bit of strength I can muster not to cry with these people every day." She sighed, lifting her head and looking around the hovel. Her gaze rested lovingly on Petula, who was snuggled like a bug in a rug, just the top of her unruly black hair visible. Kerry knew with the two thick wool blankets wrapped around her like a cocoon she was warm. For that Kerry was grateful.

"You kinda like that rug rat, don't you?"

She lifted her head and gazed at his shadowed face. "Yes, I do. Her parents are dead. I intend to keep her with me until we can find the rest of her family after this terrible crisis is over."

"And if you hadn't found her? What would have happened to her?"

Frowning, Kerry felt her appetite fade abruptly, even though her stomach was cramped and crying for food. Setting down the MRE, she whispered, "She'd probably be dead by now, because Pet couldn't scrounge enough food for herself. So many people over the last two weeks have been killed reentering their destroyed homes or a grocery store, searching for food. The quake aftershocks are powerful. Real killers. No, she'd be like a lot of others— trapped in the rubble and killed outright, or injured, with no hope of rescue."

Hanging his head, Quinn forced himself to finish his breakfast, though he was no longer hungry. "This is such a mess," he began hoarsely. "I just didn't realize the extent of it, the desperation.... Last night was bad, Kerry. As I said, I had five people— three men and two women, come to the center to steal. They were shocked to see military personnel there. It stopped them cold in their tracks."

"So, did you give them what they needed?"

Snorting softly, Quinn muttered, "First I went to the manifest inside the office to see if their names were on it, to make sure they hadn't already been given their daily ration of water and food. Once I saw they weren't listed there, I gave them supplies. Otherwise, I would have simply had to tell them that a navy helo was coming this afternoon with more supplies, and to come back after 1500 today."

Reaching out, Kerry laid her hand over his, which rested on his thick thigh. "I'm so glad you're here. I'm relieved they sent you, of all the marines available. You have a heart and soul that's in touch with the people here. Someone else might have fired at them, or denied them, but you didn't."

Her hand was warm on his, and Quinn laced his fingers through hers, giving her hand a gentle squeeze. "I have a good teacher—you." He held her gray eyes, which swam with sudden, unshed tears. How easily touched Kerry was, he was discovering. She was such a breath of life in his tight regimental world. Somehow, she was opening the door to his heart. The boldness of her touch, the coolness of her fingers made him want her even more. As his gaze moved from her eyes to her softly parted lips, the urge to lean over and kiss her nearly overwhelmed him. Kiss her? Would she allow it? Quinn thought so, judging from the warmth and admiration shining in her eyes.

Petula stirred and whimpered.

The magical moment dissolved. Instantly releasing her hand, Quinn muttered, "You'd better take care of our little rug rat."

January 15: 1600

"I can't believe this!" Kerry's voice was filled with wonder as she stood with Quinn behind the makeshift table, where several men and women were doling out food, water and medicine to needy quake victims who stood in ragged lines to receive the goods. The U.S. navy helicopter had left an hour ago, and the many supplies it brought had been carried to the center. Now, as she looked at Quinn, who stood with his usual scowl on his stony face, his M-16 resting on his right shoulder, she could barely contain her excitement.

"We've been given *three times* the amount of supplies we usually get!" she whispered. Not only that, but plenty of insulin, heart medication and antibiotics had also come with the shipment. It was like Christmas in January.

"What I like is that they're promising one flight a day by that navy helo," Quinn said. "That's even better news." He motioned with his left hand toward the waiting people, saw the hope burning in their dirty, drawn faces. Hope. Yes, the sight of those supplies made him feel good, too. His men stood at ease on either side of the table as each person approached, was looked up on the manifest, and then given supplies for the family he or she represented. Each bag given out contained bottled water, food and whatever medicine was needed.

"Yes," Kerry sighed. "But even more exciting is that the National Guard is up north of us, teamed up with Navy Seabees in huge Caterpillar bulldozers. They're beginning to open up roads into the basin!" Sighing, she added in a wobbly voice, "If they can make dirt roads into this area, that means trucks carrying supplies can get in and out. It also means ambulances and other vehicles can start taking out those most in need of medical help."

"Roads are the key," Quinn agreed. From talking to the copilot, a lieutenant by the name of Cynthia Mace, Quinn had learned that the efforts of the National Guard were going to be three-pronged. There were now enough bulldozers and navy construction personnel in place—north, south, and east—to start some major road building. Today was the kick-off date for plowing new routes through the rubble to the first four areas. Area Five wasn't targeted yet, unfortunately, for it lay at the heart of the quake zone. It was the hardest hit, and therefore would be most difficult to get to. But even though Area Five would be one of the last to get roads, the fact that the surrounding areas would soon be accessible by land vehicles meant that most of the helos could then concentrate on supplying aid to the hard-hit areas like theirs.

As well, there would be more aircraft available to
fly out serious medical cases. The hospital at Camp
Reed was chock-full. Even if a person was badly
injured, he or she would have to be flown to the
marine base first, and then to a hospital somewhere
along the West Coast. That meant an extra flight,
and right now, the airport at the base was still the
only one available, and only so much traffic could
come in and out of it. At the moment, many emergencies had to be wait-listed. But that would all
change soon, and Quinn was glad, because there
were so many people who were suffering terribly.

"Come with me," he told Kerry in a conspira-
torial tone. When she tilted her head, a question in
her gray eyes, he added, "Trust me?"

Laughing, she said, "With my life. Okay, I'll follow you."

Quinn knew she would normally stay at the center
as the distribution began, but his marines were here
to ensure the process went smoothly, quickly and
quietly. Moving out the back of the center, through
a door that hung askew on its hinges, he slipped his
hand around hers briefly, when no one could see
them.

"I have a surprise for you." Though he didn't
want to let go of her hand, he knew he had to, despite the softness he'd seen in her features when
he'd spontaneously reached out to her.

Kerry's heart skipped a beat as she hurried along
the side of the shopping center toward her home. "I

love surprises! What did you do, Quinn?'' She grinned suddenly, feeling like an elated child. Quinn made her feel so light and wonderful.

"Oh," he said teasingly, with a wolfish smile, "I had that helo bring in a couple of things for you and our rug rat. By now, Beau should have everything up and in place. Come on...."

Her shack was on the other side of the center, near a department store that had pancaked in on itself. The day had turned warm, the wind had dropped and the sun felt great on her head and shoulders. Kerry had come to appreciate the afternoon warmth as never before. As she walked, her arm sometimes brushing Quinn's, she smiled gaily. "Why do I feel like a child who is getting a surprise birthday party thrown for her?"

Chuckling, Quinn said, "Because you are. This is from me to you." As they rounded the end of the department store, he pointed toward the area where she had made her home since the earthquake had hit.

Gasping, Kerry halted. Her eyes bulged. "Oh, Quinn!" Her hands flew up to her parted lips. No more than a hundred feet away stood a large, dark green tent, erected in front of her old shelter. Lance Corporal Beau Parish came toward them, a wide smile on his face.

"Got it all done, Corporal Grayson. Just in time, I see."

"Great, Parish. Thanks. Go help one of the men

pack those grocery bags so those lines move faster now," he ordered.

"You bet." He nodded deferentially toward Kerry. "Ma'am? I hope you like what we've done." And he took off at a jog toward the center.

"What have you done?" Kerry whispered as she hurried toward the newly erected tent.

"Go look," Quinn urged, pride in his voice. He watched Kerry hurry to the tent flaps, which were open. Hearing her cry out with joy, he smiled widely.

Just seeing the blush of color sweep across Kerry's cheeks made his day. Quinn halted in front of the tent and watched her enter as if in a daze. Inside were four cots, with plenty of blankets to keep off the cold at night. The floor was a raised wooden platform, so rain would run under it and not through it, as it had in her hovel. Toward the rear was a small two-plate stove. Outside, a small gasoline-fed generator had been set up, to supply electricity for the stove as well as a small refrigerator, and best of all, a heater. The tent was snug and fully capable of withstanding the elements.

Quinn stood at the opening and watched with quiet joy as Kerry moved around inside, her hands spread open, her eyes huge as she touched everything as if to make sure it was real and not a figment of her imagination.

"I figured, since you're the leader of Area Five, you deserve to have nice digs," he said. "I talked to Morgan Trayhern a couple of days ago, and he agreed. I told him what conditions you were living in with that little girl, and he promised he'd do something worthy of your position in the community."

"Oh, Quinn!" she gasped, turning toward him. "This…this is beyond my wildest dreams! A stove! A refrigerator! That means no more fear of food poisoning!"

"Look in the fridge," he urged her quietly, stepping forward and laying his rifle on one of the cots. He sat down on the opposite cot and watched her as she knelt and slowly opened the door.

"Oh… I don't believe this!" She sat back on her haunches and looked over her shoulder at Quinn, who was smiling like the proverbial Cheshire cat. "Milk! For Petula! Oh, this is wonderful!"

"There's more…. Remember you mentioned how much you like chocolate cake? Well, you see that box in there? There's a chocolate cake in it. Morgan called up the chow hall, talked to the gunny, and they made it special—for you."

Tears flooded Kerry's eyes. She sat down and gazed in awe at the small refrigerator crammed with goodies. There was milk, yogurt, fresh eggs, at least five pounds of bacon, fresh fruit and vegetables. It was an unimaginable feast. And all because of Quinn. He missed nothing. He had heard every word she'd spoken.

Sitting there in stunned silence, her hand on the

door as she stared at the treasure trove, Kerry had no words. Her heart lifted, vibrating with such joy at his thoughtfulness that she couldn't even say thank you.

Gently closing the fridge door, she turned to him. The floor of the tent was made of thick plywood, and it was dry and solid. Placing her hand on it, she twisted around and met his half-closed eyes. He sat on the cot, his elbows resting on his thighs, his hands clasped between them. The gentle smile playing across his lips infused her with the kind of happiness she'd once felt years ago, with Lee. There was a special chemistry between her and Quinn, filling her with light and joy.

"You are…" she choked out "…incredibly wonderful. I was right, Quinn—you truly are a knight from King Arthur's round table. This is too much. Too much…"

"No, it isn't. Morgan said it for me. He said you need to start eating and sleeping regularly. You can't lead if you're weak and tired all the time, sweet pea. So now you have no excuse. You have a fridge, a stove and real food. You and our little rug rat can eat well. And when we're away from the tent, I'll post a guard to ensure no one steals anything. This belongs to you and Petula."

Whispering his name, Kerry got up off the floor. Following the promptings of her heart, she approached him and leaned down. Sliding her hands across his prickly, bearded cheeks, she framed his

face and pressed her lips against the smiling line of
his mouth. Her actions were completely spontaneous. Kerry hadn't kissed another man since Lee.
Something old and hurting dissolved in her heart as
she brushed Quinn's mouth with her own. As, after
a moment of surprise, his hands came to rest on her
shoulders.

"Thank you..." she whispered against his strong
mouth as he returned her tentative caress. "Thank
you a million times over..." And her lashes closed
as she drank deeply of his own proffered kiss. His
hands tightened on her shoulders, and Kerry relaxed.
She trusted Quinn with her life. He was giving her
life, she realized belatedly as his mouth wreaked fire
across her lips. He was just as shocked by her bold
kiss as she was, but swiftly responded with surprising tenderness.

Her world spun and dissolved beneath his mouth,
his searching exploration. Kerry knew in the back
of her mind that she shouldn't be kissing Quinn at
all, but the man deserved it. He was showing her
daily how wonderful, how sensitive and thoughtful
he was toward her and everyone else. Maybe marines were a special breed if they were all like him!

Gradually, Kerry eased away and opened her
eyes. She drowned in his smoldering blue gaze,
which spoke eloquently of his desire for her. Feeling
suddenly shaky and unsure of herself, Kerry released
him and stood up.

"I...gosh, I didn't mean to do that, Quinn...."

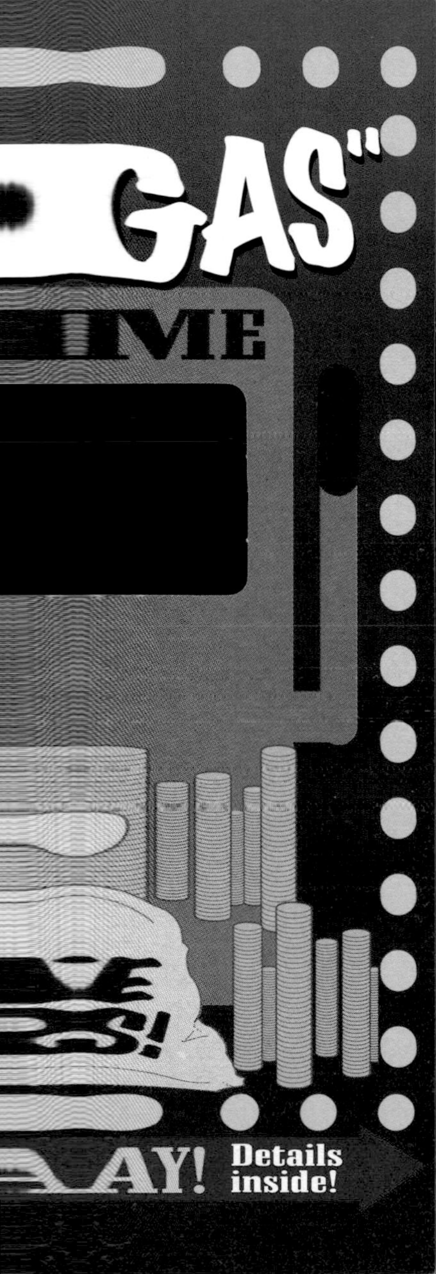
GAS"
Details inside!

FREE!
No Obligation to Buy!
No Purchase Necessary!

Play the
"LAS VEGAS" Game

YES! I have pulled back the 3 tabs. Please send me all the free Silhouette Romance® books and the gift for which I qualify. I understand that I am under no obligation to purchase any books, as explained on the back and opposite page.

315 SDL DNX4   215 SDL DNYA

FIRST NAME	LAST NAME

ADDRESS

APT.#	CITY

STATE/PROV.   ZIP/POSTAL CODE

(S-R-10/02)

7 7 7	**GET 2 FREE BOOKS & A FREE MYSTERY GIFT!**
♣ ♣ ♣	**GET 2 FREE BOOKS!**
🍒 🍒 🍒	**GET 1 FREE BOOK!**
🔔 🔔 🔔	**TRY AGAIN!**

Offer limited to one per household and not valid to current Silhouette Romance® subscribers. All orders subject to approval.

▶ DETACH AND MAIL TODAY ▶

BUSINESS REPLY MAIL

FIRST-CLASS MAIL   PERMIT NO. 717-003   BUFFALO, NY

POSTAGE WILL BE PAID BY ADDRESSEE

SILHOUETTE READER SERVICE
3010 WALDEN AVE
PO BOX 1867
BUFFALO NY 14240-9952

NO POSTAGE
NECESSARY
IF MAILED
IN THE
UNITED STATES

His brows rose. "I liked it. And I'm not sorry."

Laughing unsurely, Kerry took a step away, her hand on the tent flap. "I don't know what got into me...." She shook her head, breathless. The branding heat of his strong mouth lingered on her lips, making them tingle warmly. Deliciously.

"Are *you* sorry?" he demanded hoarsely. How beautiful she looked standing there, her hair unruly, her cheeks stained with a blush. It was her eyes, though, that told Quinn she'd enjoyed the spontaneous kiss just as much as he had.

Laughing a little, Kerry touched her brow. "No... I'm not sorry. Just shocked that I did it. This isn't like me, Quinn."

Shrugging, he felt a grin crawl across his mouth. He could still taste the sweetness of Kerry on his lips. "Maybe it's the times. The pressure. Who knows? One thing I do know, though, sweet pea— I'm not sorry it happened."

Chapter Six

January 16: 0630

"I don't want you to go with me," Quinn said in a low voice outside the tent the next morning. Dawn was just crawling across the eastern horizon. Above him the last of the inky darkness was fleeing before the coming sun.

"Too bad. I'm going with you, Quinn, so stop being so protective, okay?" Kerry, too, kept her voice low. The morning was crisp and chilly. Today she was wearing her new marine cammo jacket and she felt much warmer—thanks to Quinn, who had radioed in for extra warm clothing for so many in Area Five. He had made sure she got a jacket, as well.

Pulling her away from the tent, where Petula and Sylvia were still sleeping, Quinn scowled. Yesterday, he'd tried to persuade Kerry not to come with him as he began to hunt for Diablo. She'd balked then, as she was doing now. After that soft, unexpected kiss, he found himself not wanting to put her in the line of fire for any reason. He had slept restlessly last night on his new cot, beneath several blankets. Kerry had asked him to stay with them. He knew Diablo was around and the new tents might draw their interest. The heater had warmed them all, and he'd noticed that Kerry, Petula and Sylvia all slept deeply and soundly. Usually, they were cold beneath their threadbare blankets and moved sporadically to keep warm.

"No one knows Diablo better than me," Kerry told him with grim determination. She pulled the pistol she carried from the black holster at her right hip. Checking it to make sure a bullet was in the chamber, she replaced the safety and strapped it back in place. "And in your uniform, you'll be a prime target for those guys. They hate authority."

"Like they won't spot you, too?"

She grinned as they stepped farther away from the tent. "Well, since I'm wearing this marine jacket, they'll probably think I'm one of you. Either way, it doesn't matter, Quinn. We're both targets, because we represent authority. I've tangled three times with members of this group since the quake hit, and believe me, they take no prisoners. You've seen that from the reports I've made. I've attempted in every case to talk to witnesses who were there. We've gotten some names. After this disaster is over, I intend to hang these guys in a court of law. They're not going to get away with these atrocities.''

''They're already up on murder charges for two marine helo pilots.'' Halting, Quinn slung his small knapsack, filled with water and food for a day's worth of hunting, across his shoulders. Picking up the M-16, he switched the safety off, then kept the barrel pointed downward, the gun ready to fire in his hand.

''I know,'' Kerry whispered sadly. ''Can I help you carry anything?''

Giving her a dark look, he growled, ''You aren't going to stay behind, are you?''

''No.''

''Sometimes I wish you could be like other women,'' he groused, his umber brows dipping.

''Ouch. That sounds so old-fashioned to me. Didn't your hill women do anything but stay home and raise the kids?'' she teased lightly as they began to walk toward a flattened neighborhood ahead.

''My sister, Katie, is a crack shot. She always went with Pa and me, and usually ended up bringing home more squirrels for the stew than either of us.''

''And is Katie married now?''

''Nope. She went on to Glen, Kentucky, the closest town out of the mountains where our clan lives, and got an education like I did. She's a teacher now," he said proudly. "The first in our family to get a college diploma. They built a small school for the hill children about five years ago, and she teaches there."

"I see. So not all hill women are expected to just stay at home and do domestic things?"

Giving her a disgruntled look, Quinn said, "No. But it's still…odd when they don't."

"Hmm, odd as in bad? Or odd as in unique and apart from what most other women do?" She flashed him a smile, warmly recalling his heated, hungry mouth upon hers. Kerry had slept deeply last night, partly because she'd been warm for the first time since the quake hit, with that wonderful heater in the tent. Last night, she'd dreamed of Quinn. He was making love to her in a glade deep in the mountains, near a pool. It was wonderful, so primal and natural. Kerry wasn't about to tell him that, however. The look in his normally glacial blue eyes had changed. That kiss she'd given him had changed everything, she was discovering. Was that what she wanted? Had she kissed Quinn because of her own shock and trauma over the quake? To alleviate some of the stress from the horrendous responsibility she carried daily? Or was it out of relief at having a partner who would help shoulder it all? Kerry was uncertain.

She was still letting go of Lee, of their wonderful marriage. Grief didn't just suddenly end a year after your spouse died, Kerry had discovered. Her emotions were like a roller coaster, going up and down. When grief surfaced, she felt it for days or weeks, and then it would submerge again, and she'd be okay about going on alone once more.

Quinn noticed the faraway look in Kerry's face as they left the shopping center and walked carefully along a chewed-up asphalt avenue toward a long line of stucco homes that lay in shambles. In front of each home, families still slept in whatever makeshift shelter they had pulled together.

"You seem far away," he noted.

"Sorry... I was thinking, Quinn. Did you answer my question?"

"Not yet. I just felt you leave me."

A little stunned by his admission, she gave him a look of surprise. "Are you psychic or something? I did go away. I was thinking of the past."

Shrugging, he trudged down the middle of what had once been a street. "I've been accused of having a strong sixth sense. Pa said all good hunters have that gift," he said, studying the trees that had once lined the area, now ripped out of the ground and lying around like scattered toothpicks. Downed power lines and poles looked like giant spiderwebs where they crisscrossed. There was no electricity in the lines—good news, because the dark cables snaked across collapsed roofs and dusty yellow lawns.

Impressed, Kerry asked, "You have this skill with everyone? Your fire team?"

Feeling a little self-conscious, Quinn held her interested gray gaze. "Not with everyone. Just... special people, I guess."

"Well," she teased softly, "it's nice to be one of those special people in your life."

Caught off guard by her tender admission, Quinn studied her candid expression, before his gaze roamed over her face, her hair. This morning, Kerry's locks were washed and brushed. He'd made sure that toiletry items were on board that U.S. Navy helicopter, too. Now he saw that her sable hair actually had reddish highlights in it. Yesterday, for the first time, Kerry had washed her hair in a basin of precious water. Petula had gotten her hair scrubbed as well. It had done Quinn's heart good to see them smiling and laughing as Kerry had gently towel-dried Petula's long, black hair, the child seated in her lap. It was then that he knew Kerry would be a good mother.

By the time they'd passed the first two blocks of the neighborhood, it was 0600 and the sky was brightening in the east. There was no wind this morning, and Kerry was grateful. She pulled a map of the region out of the large pocket of her oversize cammo jacket.

Quinn kept looking around, on guard, the rifle clasped in his hands. Members of the Diablo gang weren't going to be easily distinguished from the people of Area Five. They were dressed just like them. The only thing that made them stand out was that, upon occasion, they wore a white headband. If the leader, a man named Snake Williams, was smart, he'd have his survivalists fade into the local population so none could be singled out. Quinn wasn't so sure Snake was that smart, but he wouldn't bet the farm that he wasn't.

According to Kerry's reports, Snake was the man's nickname. Helluva nickname, Quinn thought. No one knew his real name. But in the second incident report, one of the victims remembered hearing another gang member use his last name: Williams. The victim, a woman whose teenage son had been taken hostage, a gun held to his head by Snake as he demanded all the food she'd managed to retrieve from her destroyed home, had given the leader everything. Her son had lived.

Kerry folded the map into a small square as they continued down the next block. The street was in fist-size pieces of asphalt, and she had to be careful where she stepped, or she'd fall and hurt herself.

"So where did you go before, when you had that faraway look in your eyes?" Quinn asked now.

"Where did I go?" She looked at him and smiled slightly. "I was thinking of how I boldly kissed you the other day. It wasn't like me, and I was wondering where that spontaneity came from.'' Coming to a stop at the end of the block, she looked around, getting her bearings with the map in her hands. Quinn halted at her shoulder, less than a foot from her. She liked the feeling of protection he always gave her.

"Are you sorry it happened?'' he asked as he watched her run her index finger along the route they were taking. Holding his breath momentarily, he hoped that she wasn't feeling regret. Why did he want that kiss to mean something beyond what it probably was? Kerry had been thrilled over the gift of the tent. It was possible she had just kissed him out of gratitude. Quinn was bothered by the fact he wanted it to mean more than that.

Looking up at Quinn's recently shaved face, Kerry savored his embracing blue gaze. "I don't know any other way to be than honest, Quinn. So here goes....'' She took a deep breath. "I surprised myself by going over and kissing you. No, I don't regret it. But I'm scared, too. That wasn't like me. I keep trying to figure out why I did it. Was it because of the stress of the quake? Shock?'' Lifting her fingers, she tunneled them through her hair in a nervous motion. "I haven't been attracted to any man since Lee died.''

Though he nodded, Quinn felt his heart sinking. Quirking her lips, Kerry refolded the map and slid it back into the pocket of her jacket. "It's you, Quinn. Whatever that means, it's you. I wanted to kiss you. I like being with you. I like the way you think. Most of all, I like how you treat others. You're a true leader. You listen to your men and their ideas. You don't rule by control, you rule by soliciting their opinions, respecting their insights and experiences before you make a decision."

"And that's important to you, Kerry?"

She smiled hesitantly. "Yes…yes, it is." Opening her hands, which now had warm gloves on them, thanks to Quinn, she said, "You've surprised me, Quinn. When Morgan Trayhern said there was a Marine Corps fire team coming in here, I had this idea that you were all John Wayne, gung-ho warriors who would look at us civilians like a plague that had to be cured." Her smiled widened. "But you didn't."

"We're trained for suburban warfare," he told her seriously. "Morgan said you had the goods. You were our contact. No one knows this area better than you because you've been clawing out a life here for two weeks before we arrived. What else could I do but listen to you? Learn from you?" She was achingly beautiful as the first rays of sun shot over the horizon and touched her slightly curled, short brown hair. Once again he could see the reddish highlights, and he had a maddening urge to run his hands through the silky strands. How badly he wanted to reach out and touch Kerry.

Laughing shortly, she said, "I found that out." Her lips pulled in at the corners as she studied his frowning countenance. "I'm finding myself really attracted to you, Quinn." There, the truth was out on the table. She saw his brows raise in surprise, and then his blue eyes narrowed speculatively on her. A delightful river of warmth coursed through her heart and down into her lower body. Kerry recognized that look: it was desire. For her and her alone. Ordinarily, if a man gazed at her that way, she ignored him. But not now. Not with Quinn. Instead, Kerry absorbed his look like a starving animal.

"I guess I'm just realizing how lonely I really was," she admitted in a low tone. "After Lee died, well, I threw myself into my work at the sheriff's office. I ran a teenage drug program for the county, too, so it kept me extra busy. I didn't want to go home at night to our house. I didn't want the silence warring with my memories. It was…just too much for me to bear…so I kept super busy to take the edge off my grief and loss."

"I can understand that," Quinn said. He saw the grief in her eyes and grasped as never before what the loss of a loved one could do to a person.

"Have you ever lost someone you loved, Quinn?" She earnestly searched his scowling face.

There was such tenderness in this marine who stood inches from her. Kerry ached to throw her arms around him, kiss him and lose herself in his embrace.

"No...not really. My parents are still alive. All us kids are alive. I had my grandpa die, and that was hard on me. They lived in the holler down from our cabin, and he was an important part of my life." Looking up, Quinn saw a flight of birds wing overhead on their way toward the Pacific Ocean in the distance. They were seagulls, their white plumage shining in the rising sun. Gazing back at Kerry, he said, "But losing someone I loved and lived with? No."

"I don't wish it on anyone," Kerry whispered forcefully. "Even this quake, Quinn, is peanuts compared to the emotional mountains and valleys I've been moving through since I lost Lee."

Reaching out, he brushed her cheek. Kerry's skin was smooth, like a warm, fuzzy peach beneath his fingertips. "Thanks for telling me where you went. It helps me to understand you." *And appreciate you.* But Quinn didn't say that.

"I haven't met many women who are as honest as you are, sweet pea." The endearment rolled off his tongue. He saw Kerry's eyes widen momentarily at his grazing touch, and then her cheek became stained with pink. He positively itched to touch her again, touch her longer, and in a way that showed her what lay in his rapidly beating heart.

What was happening? Was it her? This disaster? Quinn wasn't at all sure. What he was sure of was that Kerry touched his heart big time, and his desire for her was escalating. It was so unexpected that Quinn didn't know what to do about it. In a way, he felt helpless around her. Not that Kerry flirted with him or egged him on. He'd see that warm look in her eyes from time to time when he caught her watching him in a quiet moment, but that was all. She hadn't tried to kiss him again, rub up against him or find an excuse to touch him.

Managing a crooked smile, Kerry whispered, "I like being called sweet pea. That must be a hill expression?"

Chuckling and a little embarrassed, he said, "Yeah, it is. My grandpa called my grandmother by that name for as long as I could recall. I guess…" he paused, searching for the right words "…you remind me of her. She's a gutsy old lady in her seventies now, and I've always admired her spunk and rebellious nature."

"I'm rebellious?" There was a teasing note in Kerry's tone. How she ached to have Quinn touch her unexpectedly like that again.

He shrugged. "Maybe. I don't know of any hill women who are in law enforcement. You broke the mold, as we'd say, Kerry. But I don't see that as bad. Just different." And wonderful. She was special to him, though he was afraid to ask himself why.

"Just don't call me by that name in front of anyone, okay? I've got a job to do and a reputation to uphold. Somehow, a sheriff's deputy being called sweet pea could be counterproductive."

Joining her laughter, Quinn looked around. "Yeah, don't worry. I won't undermine your reputation or rank. Come on, let's head east, toward the borderland region where Area Six butts up against us."

Nodding, Kerry fell into step at his side. By now, the whole neighborhood was awakening. Small campfires to cook on were in evidence on the lawns in front of the houses, the inhabitants huddled around them for warmth. Her heart, however, was pulsing with a need for more conversation with Quinn. Kerry sighed inwardly. Was it possible to fall in love with someone so quickly?

Chapter Seven

January 16: 1500

It was near 1500 when they unexpectedly ran into the Diablo gang. Near the boundary with Area Six was a row of suburban homes only partially destroyed by the quake. Some were still intact. Quinn knew by now that a standing house meant many things to a quake victim: a way to get clothes, stored food or water, plus a roof overhead, providing there weren't large cracks running through the structure. The lucky person who had a standing or even partially standing house was a drawing card for others. Quinn had found out from Kerry as they'd walked through the devastated neighborhoods that frequently many families would gather and use that home as a central focus point for their small community. And at night, providing the house was stable, as many as forty or fifty people would crowd into the rooms and hallways to sleep, to escape the raw January elements.

The afternoon sun was strong and warm. Quinn had stuffed his and Kerry's jackets in the pack he carried on his shoulders, but was still sweating freely. The flak vest beneath his cammo shirt chafed him so badly with each movement that he wanted to tear the thing off, but didn't.

They had just come to the last square block of a neighborhood that butted up against the Area Six boundary. Three homes were standing. Kerry held out her hand to stop him. Her brows moved downward.

"Wait…" she cautioned.

"What?" Quinn saw she was studying a crowd that stood in a semicircle in front of one of the homes. At least thirty people were riveted in place, looking at something he couldn't see.

"Trouble," Kerry whispered in warning, unstrapping her pistol from her holster. "I think it's Diablo…."

Though he didn't know how she knew that, Quinn didn't question her. Immediately he locked and loaded his M-16, after taking off the safety. But before he could intercede, gunfire erupted near them. Six geysers of dirt sprayed up at their feet, the bullets narrowly missing them.

There was no time to think, only to react. Quinn saw Kerry dive for the ground, aiming her pistol to the left of the crowd.

As he lunged for the ground in turn, because there was nowhere to hide, he saw a tall, swarthy-looking man coming at them, a submachine gun in his hand. The winking red-and-yellow flashes from his gun barrel told Quinn that he was firing directly at them. Quinn grunted and rolled to the left. The man was in back of the crowd. Quinn couldn't return fire for fear of wounding a civilian. *Damn!*

Kerry? Where was she? Jerking his head to the right, Quinn spotted a car that had been upended. Leaping to his feet, he caught sight of her in his peripheral vision. She was running out in the open, pistol held in her right hand, her entire focus on the Diablo member coming at them, rifle blazing.

Bullets whined and whistled around Quinn. He had to find protection or he was going to be hit! Digging in the toes of his black leather boots, he sprinted toward the car, which was a hundred feet away.

"Get down! Get down!"

Kerry's voice carried loudly across the area.

Somewhere in Quinn's mind, he knew she was screaming at the civilians to duck so that she or Quinn could take a clean shot at their attacker. He had no time to look. Bullets whined past his head. Dirt leaped up near his right foot as he dived the last ten feet to the car.

With one final leap, Quinn landed heavily in the dirt and rolled. He was safe! Once behind the car, he scrambled upward. Where was the shooter? Where? His heart was pounding. Sweat was stinging in his eyes. Searching frantically, he heard the screams and shouts of the people. He saw them falling to the earth, hugging it and screaming out in fear.

It was then that his blood turned cold. He saw three more of the Diablo members, all wearing white headbands, at the center of the group of people. They were heavily armed.

Looking to his right once more, he spotted Kerry. His heart shrieked out in protest. She was out in the open, with no place to hide! His mouth dropped open as she sank down on one knee, steadied her pistol in both hands and fired directly at the three members.

Cursing, Quinn focused on the first Diablo and squeezed off three shots. The man went down, his submachine gun flying out of his hands. It landed harmlessly five feet away on the chewed-up street.

Kerry! Heart pounding with fear because she was a fully exposed target, Quinn steadied the rifle against the top of the car. To his horror, two of the thugs were firing at her. He saw one jerk and fly backward. Kerry had gotten him. One more to go!

Breathing hard, Quinn sighted on the big guy with red hair who was focused so intently on Kerry. There wasn't more than three hundred feet between the two of them. Squeezing off a shot, Quinn aimed for the man's bare head. He couldn't be careless. If he was, he might kill one of the civilians flattened on the lawn near where the man stood.

Kerry! In that split second before he brushed the trigger of his rifle, Quinn knew she was in trouble. She was an easy target.

Kerry kept her wits about her, despite the shrieks and screams of people surrounding her. This was the only angle to shoot the thug. The gunfire was deafening. She knew she was a target. She didn't want to die, but they were firing at her with a hailstorm of bullets.

There was no time to worry about Quinn. She'd seen him dive for safety behind the overturned auto. Good! As she steadied herself on one knee and held her pistol firm, she fired off shot after shot. They had to be head shots, because if she aimed lower one of her bullets might strike a civilian. And that would be unforgivable.

A bullet slammed into her right thigh. At first, Kerry felt only a vague, stinging heat there. She was too focused, her adrenaline pumping too strongly, to feel anything more. She saw two Diablo members go down. Satisfaction thrummed through her. *Good!* More people shrieked as the man fell on top of them, unconscious. One more to go.

It was then, as Kerry squeezed off the ninth shot from her pistol, that a bullet struck her in the head.

She didn't even see that her last bullet missed her attacker as she fell back.

No! Oh, God, no! Quinn saw Kerry crumple. He saw the pistol fall nervelessly from her fingers. She sagged backward, like a rag doll, limp and lifeless. With his last shot, he took out the last member of Diablo. The man crumpled to the ground, his weapon falling from his hands.

Leaping from behind the auto, Quinn sprinted toward where Kerry lay. She was on her back, her body twisted, her arms thrown outward. Sobbing for breath, his chest hurting, Quinn cried out her name as he dropped to his knees beside her.

Around him, people were starting to get up and move. Children were crying. Women were sobbing. All his focus, his heart—his life—centered on Kerry. Dropping his weapon, Quinn went into EMT mode. The A, B, Cs—airway, breathing and circulation—roared through his fragmented mind. He saw blood staining her dark green slacks on her right thigh. Worse, he saw blood on the right temple of her head. She was pale, seemingly lifeless.

Thrusting his hand out, he put his shaking fingers on her pulse. Yes! She was alive! *Thank God. Thank God.* He leaned down, trying to still his chaotic breathing in order to hear, and placed his ear near her nostrils. Was that a faint puff of air? She was still breathing! She was alive! But would she live?

Gripping the computerized radio he carried,

Quinn punched in the code to connect him with the medevac helicopter base. It was a special frequency that would tie in directly to Camp Reed, to a Blackhawk helicopter on loan from the U.S. Army, that sat waiting for just such a call from military personnel in the field. Glancing down at Kerry's soft, pale face, her slack lips, the thick dark lashes against her cheeks, Quinn felt his whole world tilt out of control.

People were running over to him, crowding around him, asking if they could help. Quinn shook his head. He waited what seemed hours for the medevac team to answer. When they did, he gave them coordinates.

"Hurry! She's critical. It's a head wound!" His voice cracked. Everything blurred as Quinn signed off. It would be fifteen minutes before the chopper arrived—the worst, most nightmarish fifteen minutes of his life as he leaned down and continued to assess her condition.

He felt the touch of a man's hand on his shoulder. Someone was thrusting a blanket forward, to keep Kerry warm. Trying not to sob, Quinn looked up—into the terrorized faces of the civilians who surrounded them.

"Y-you saved us," a woman choked out. She gripped her small boy in her arms. "Those men were from Diablo. They were going to kill my baby here, for food. Oh, thank you...thank you!" She began to weep harder.

Quinn put his hands up. "Please," he called, "give us some room. There's nothing you can do here—unless there's a medical doctor present?" He prayed there would be.

The people stood mute, staring down at him and at one another, their faces mirroring shock from this latest tragedy.

No one answered, so Quinn quickly went back to work. Inside his pack, he carried a small EMT kit for just such emergencies. Because Kerry had a head wound, it was important not to raise her feet. Ordinarily, when a person was unconscious and in shock, that's exactly what was done, to force the blood back toward the head and into the major organs of the body. But not this time.

Reaching out, he touched her curly brown hair, which glinted with red highlights from the slanting sun. Shaking his head, Quinn tried to think. But he couldn't. As he knelt at her side and applied a pressure bandage to the bullet wound in her right thigh, he wanted to scream—scream in pure frustration. Kerry couldn't die. She just couldn't!

January 16: 1700

"How is she?"

Quinn turned toward the deep male voice. He was standing alone in the surgery floor waiting room. Looking up, he recognized Morgan Trayhern coming toward him, his black brows knitted, his blue eyes narrowed with concern.

Opening his hands, Quinn whispered, "I don't know, sir. She's been in surgery for an hour now. The paramedic on board the Blackhawk said the wound on her thigh was clean and superficial. It's her head. She took a shot to the head." Numbly, Quinn sat down. He didn't know what else to do. He felt so damned helpless. Kerry's blood was on his shirt. On his hands. Her head wound had bled profusely, as that type always did—even when he'd helped the paramedic take care of her in the chopper on the way back to the base.

Morgan gripped his slumped shoulder. "Damn, I'm sorry, Quinn." He sat down with him on one of the red plastic chairs. "Tell me what happened?"

Quinn knew it took an act of Congress to get Morgan out of Logistics; the man was busier than anyone at Camp Reed. The fact that he was here made a powerful statement about him. Morgan cared deeply for the people in the field.

Swallowing hard, Quinn rubbed his face. Hot, unexpected tears jammed into his eyes. He looked down so Trayhern couldn't see them. Opening his mouth, he tried to gather his shocked, fragmented thoughts. He knew Morgan was expecting a report. Emotionally, Quinn wasn't with it. His heart was with Kerry in the surgery room.

"Take your time," Morgan said heavily, studying

his profile. He saw the glitter of tears in Quinn's eyes even though he tried to hide them.

Finally, Quinn managed to get ahold of himself. He sat there and talked in a rough whisper, his legs spread, his hands gripped between them. When he finished, he heard Morgan curse softly beneath his breath.

"This gang is a helluva lot stronger and more violent than we realized," he told Quinn. "We're getting reports from other areas of their activity. It's a much larger group than we realized. And there's no way a fire team is going to handle this volatile situation. There's just too many of them." He scratched his head and muttered, "I'm going to have to put together a special Recon team with a doctor in case of medical casualties, and have them find the bastards."

"Sir, what with all the needs and demands of the people in Kerry's area, we're stretched too thin." Quinn opened his hands. "This was the first day since our arrival that she and I were out reconnoitering the area. I hadn't expected to run into them. We were undermanned. We didn't have enough firepower. And they had civilians they were using as a shield so we couldn't fire back. They knew what they were doing."

"I hear you, Quinn. Damn, I hear you." Morgan sighed and stood up. "Listen, you go get cleaned up. I've arranged for you to have a room at the

B.O.Q. Take a hot shower. There will be a fresh set of clothes for you, Son.''

Looking up in surprise, Quinn muttered, ''The B.O.Q., sir?'' That was the Bachelor Officers Quarters, and only officers were allowed to stay there. Not an enlisted person like him.

He saw Morgan smile grimly. ''You're getting a field commission, Corporal. As of right now, I'm making you a second lieutenant. Orders just came down today that we're to pinpoint marines with leadership qualities out there in the field and promote them battlefield rank. Okay?''

In shock, Quinn sat there, his mouth open. He didn't know what to say. He saw dark satisfaction glimmer in Morgan's eyes.

''There will be a set of silver bars with your clean clothes, Lieutenant. I suggest you get over there, clean up and hotfoot it back here.'' Morgan glanced at his watch. ''I'm late for a meeting. I'll try to swing back by here in two hours. Just know there's a lot of people praying for Kerry right now, Son. I know how much she means to you. I see it in your face, hear it in your voice. Let's hope for the best....''

Stunned with the good news that warred against his worry and anguish, Quinn sat there for a long time trying to digest it all. During a war, it wasn't uncommon for an enlisted person to be handed officer's rank. This quake, the horrific magnitude of destruction, was a war, he realized belatedly. And

Morgan Trayhern had just made him a second lieutenant. My God.

Shaking his head, Quinn shuffled stiffly out of the
visitors' center and to the nurses' station, a beehive
of activity. He caught one nurse's attention and
asked her about Kerry.

"Hey, look, Corporal, I don't know. She's in operating theater three, that's all I can tell you." Harried, she grabbed a clipboard. "You'll just have to
wait."

Nodding and swallowing hard, Quinn turned
woodenly toward the elevators at the end of the
highly polished white passageway. Right now, all
he wanted to do was hold Kerry's hand. To whisper
to her that she would be all right. In a daze, he
walked unsteadily toward the row of elevators. The
hallway was crowded with male and female nurses
in light blue uniforms hurrying in and out of surgical
rooms where patients lay. The antiseptic odors were
cloying and sharp. As an EMT, Quinn knew what
went on in an operating room. Kerry would be on a
table surrounded by hospital staff, a doctor heading
up the team trying to save her life.

Quinn's mind gyrated with grief. With fear. Kerry
couldn't die! She just couldn't! As he pressed the
down button, the door to one elevator slid open and
he stepped in. There were five other people, all in
cammos, standing there, their faces grim. A gurney
bearing an older woman covered with blankets stood

beside them. A hospital corpsman held up a bag for the IV flowing into her right arm.

The intense anguish he felt for Kerry nearly suffocated Quinn. As the elevator dropped to the first-floor lobby of the huge naval hospital, he couldn't wait to get out of there, and escaped hurriedly into the cool evening air. The sun was just setting. Standing on the cracked sidewalk, Quinn barely noticed the people milling around him like ceaseless droves of busy ants. Instead, his gaze sought out the B.O.Q.

It felt so strange to be heading toward officers' quarters. He'd been given a battlefield commission! Quinn had never expected that, not in a million years. It just wasn't done. The last time that had occurred was during the Vietnam War, when so many young officers were killed because they were unprepared for jungle warfare. And without an officer to lead, the entire unit ground to a halt. Now Quinn was an officer.

None of it really mattered, he thought as he headed to the B.O.Q., his heart heavy with worry over Kerry. To his surprise, his name was already on the register at the front desk. The clerk handed him a key to a room on the second floor, no questions asked. Quinn knew he looked filthy, what with Kerry's blood staining the front of his cammos. He climbed the stairs slowly, in shock, then went through the motions of finding the small room. Opening the door, he found a queen-size bed with a floral bedspread, and a set of maple dressers. The curtains at the window matched the bedspread. Different rooms were available. Some were suites and others were not. He was grateful to have any room.

Standing there, he felt torn apart. The world he'd just left was so devastated, this one so neat, clean and sparkling, with all the amenities. There was a pitcher of ice water on the coffee table in front of the leather davenport. Water! It was so desperately needed out there in the heart of the quake zone, and here it was readily available. There were so many thirsty and dehydrated people out there, many dying slowly from a lack of water. He felt as if he were in a surreal nightmare as he stared down at the pitcher. Walking past it, Quinn headed directly to the bathroom. How wonderful a hot, steamy shower would feel.

As he climbed out of his dirty uniform and let it fall on the tile floor, he thought of Kerry. She hadn't had a shower in weeks. Guilt ate at him as he stepped into the glass cubicle and felt the first hot droplets fall. As he applied soap to a washcloth, he wished desperately with all his heart and soul, that Kerry could be here with him. He wanted to wash her gently, kiss her, caress her and tell her how much she meant to him.

Standing in the pummeling stream of hot water, Quinn began to cry. He'd never done that before— cry on the spur of the moment. The experience was foreign to him. The salty tears flooding down his heavily bearded face mingled with the heated water from the showerhead above. He had no idea how the tears had started—or why. All he knew as he stood there, feet apart, the water running over him, was that he'd fallen helplessly in love with Kerry. She was an extraordinary person, so very courageous, and yet incredibly kind and compassionate. As Quinn savagely rubbed his face with the soapy cloth to erase the unbidden tears leaking out of his eyes, he felt a wave of sheer terror tunneling through his chest. Kerry didn't know how he felt about her. Quinn hadn't wanted to admit the feelings growing powerfully toward her. Not even to himself.

He'd shrugged off his feelings as something that had grown out of the trauma of the quake. But now he knew differently, and it hurt that he'd never told her. It felt as if someone was slicing up his heart with a razor blade, one deep, violent cut after another.

What if Kerry died on the surgery table? What if she became paralyzed or worse, a vegetable, because of the bullet? A beautiful life destroyed by a roving band of thugs... It wasn't fair, Quinn thought as he stood there, gasping for breath. He tried again to stop his tears, but it was impossible.

If someone had been in the bedroom, they would have heard a man sobbing hard and long. But no one was there to hear him. The sounds of his grief, of his hopes and dreams for a life with Kerry were all muffled by the walls.

Would Kerry live or die? The question tore at Quinn, and not even his tears brought him any relief.

Chapter Eight

"How long are they going to keep Kerry in an induced coma?" Laura Trayhern asked. She sat in the wheelchair, Baby Jane wrapped in her arms.

Quinn sat on a red vinyl lounge chair, tension filling him. "I just talked to Dr. Edmonds. She was the surgeon for Kerry." Rubbing his bloodshot eyes, he felt fear clawing at his throat. He tried to keep his voice even and detached. Just the look on Laura's kind face broke something loose within him. Even though she was confined to a wheelchair because of the broken ankle she'd sustained during the earthquake, she had made an effort to come up and visit him. Her kindness overwhelmed him.

"And Dr. Edmonds said they were going to purposely keep Kerry unconscious with drugs?"

Nodding, Quinn muttered, "She said something about Kerry's skull being cracked. The bullet glanced off her cranium and cracked it. The doc is worried that her brain will swell because of the injury."

"I see...." Laura sighed. "But Kerry's brain is okay? The bullet didn't penetrate?"

Releasing his own trembling sigh, Quinn said, "No, thank God, it didn't, Mrs. Trayhern."

"Call me Laura." She smiled softly. "Then there's a lot of good to come out of this? The doctor is inducing her coma so her brain doesn't swell?"

"Something like that," Quinn murmured. He was exhausted. Even now, he wasn't thinking clearly. The surgery had taken five hours. He'd come straight back to the hospital after cleaning up and donning his fresh cammos, with the single black bar which was seen on each shoulder to denote his new second lieutenant status. Then he'd had to wait for Dr. Edmonds to finally appear and tell him how Kerry was doing.

Reaching out, Laura squeezed his arm. "I can tell you're tired, Quinn. Have you seen Kerry yet?"

"No, I haven't. She's in recovery right now, and no one's allowed in. They'll transfer her to ICU, the critical care unit, in about thirty minutes." He looked down at the watch on his hairy wrist. Feeling as if he were moving through a nightmare, Quinn sighed again. All he wanted was to see Kerry. To touch her. To convince himself that she was still alive. She *had* to live! She just had to! Clenching his teeth against the avalanche of wild, frightening thoughts, he glanced over at Laura. She was holding the baby in her arms, looking content and at peace.

The thought that Kerry would look like that with their baby struck him full force. He sat back in amazement. Quinn had no idea where *that* errant idea had come from. He knew he was sleep deprived. Knew that the emotional burden of Kerry's wounds weighed heavier on him than anything he'd ever encountered. Wrestling with all of it, Quinn felt like he was being torn apart, piece by piece, and he didn't know where to go or what to do with all those emotions.

"Listen," Laura whispered gently, "I know you want to wait until she's transferred to ICU, so you can see her…touch her and know that she's alive. But after that, Quinn, go back to your room at the B.O.Q. and sleep. You look like you're in shock yourself."

With a low, startled laugh, Quinn said, "Yeah… I am. I'm a trained EMT and I recognize my own symptoms, Laura." It was easy to be on a first-name basis with Laura Trayhern. She was so warm and caring. No wonder Morgan loved her. In many respects Kerry was very much like Laura, Quinn thought as he sat there holding her warm gaze. They both had that gentle nurturing quality.

"I promise to get some rest soon," he told her gravely.

"Morgan said that he's in contact with Sergeant Slater, the leader of the platoon your fire team came from. They're sending out a replacement for you now. That should make you feel better."

"It does, thanks. But all those people in Area Five will wonder about Kerry. They love her. They've come to rely on her—a *lot*. I need to get back out there...."

"In time," Laura counseled wisely. "First things first, Quinn. Make sure Kerry is okay, and then get some badly needed sleep. Morgan said for you to come to his office over in Logistics at 0900 tomorrow morning. Until then, you have nothing but downtime on your hands."

Nodding, Quinn whispered, "Thanks...."

Just then, a nurse in a light blue smock came into the visiting room.

"Corporal Grayson?" She frowned and looked at him again, studying his clean uniform and the bars on his shoulders. "Er... I'm sorry, Lieutenant Grayson? Deputy Kerry Chelton has been transferred to ICU. Mr. Trayhern said the two of you are engaged, so that makes you family. Only family members are allowed to see her at this point." The nurse looked at her watch. "You have five minutes every hour with her, sir. That's the rule."

Quinn rose to his feet, feeling uneasy with his

new rank. One moment enlisted, the next an officer. He had seen the brunette corpsman's eyes widen as she saw the lieutenant's bars on the cammo shirt he wore. "I understand. Thank you," he told her.

"No problem, sir." She turned and hurried away.

Quinn turned to Laura. "Thanks to you…and your husband. I don't know what I'd do right now if you hadn't been here."

Grinning slightly, Laura rocked the baby in the pink blanket gently. The little tyke was sound asleep. "I told Morgan he'd better concoct a story so you could get in to see Kerry. Patients in ICU aren't allowed visits from 'friends.' I wasn't sure you knew that, so I told Morgan to tell the nursing staff you two were engaged." She looked up at him, her eyes sparkling. "I hope that doesn't bother you, Quinn?"

Reaching out, he touched her shoulder. "No, ma'am, it doesn't. I'm not thinking fast on my feet at this point, and I'm grateful you are. Right now, all I want—need—is to see Kerry…."

"Then," Laura whispered, "go see her. And remember, even though a person is in a coma, they can still *hear* you. That's a medical fact. So go in there and *talk* to her. She'll be listening, Quinn. I know she will."

Swallowing hard, he lifted his fingers from Laura's slim shoulder. "Do you need help first, though? I know you came up here on your own."

Laughing, Laura said, "If you could ask the orderly who is waiting at the nurse's desk to take me back to my room, I'd appreciate it, Quinn. Thanks for asking."

Nodding, Quinn felt his heart begin to thud with dread. "I'll get him right now and then I'll go see Kerry. And I'll see Morgan tomorrow at 0900. Thanks—for everything…"

He left, walking almost woodenly. The passageway was clogged with orderlies and nurses hurrying in and out of rooms where so many injured and sick people lay. Keeping near the wall, Quinn moved like a robot toward the nurses' station where he asked the awaiting orderly to take Laura back to her room. Then he turned and headed to ICU, which was at the other end of the surgical floor. Kerry. He was going to see Kerry, finally….

The nursing station at ICU was filled with quiet tension. A red-haired corpswave behind the desk pulled Kerry's board off a hook.

"It says here that you're her fiancé, Lieutenant Grayson?" she asked, checking the second page of the document.

"Yes…yes, I am." It was a lie, but he wished it was true.

"Okay, no problem. She's in ICU 4. Just walk down there." She pointed behind her. "You have five minutes. I'll have to come and get you should you go over that time limit." Giving him a harried look, she added, "How about I leave it up to you to know when your time is up? We're busy, as you can see, so if you could…?"

"Sure, no problem," he promised her.

"Great. Go ahead, sir."

Turning, Quinn hurried toward the passageway. There were four ICU rooms, each walled with glass so that the nursing staff could see at a glance how a patient was doing. Kerry's room was on the right, the number 4 mounted in gold on the glass panel. Anxiously, he looked at her. She was propped up on a bed, with so many tubes running into her mouth, nose and arms that it scared him.

Opening the door quietly, Quinn was hit with the powerful smell of antiseptic, so strong it made him nauseous. Standing there, he eyed all the equipment on either side of the bed where Kerry lay without moving. She was on complete life support, a machine pumping for her, to mimic her breathing. Every few seconds the light blue covering across Kerry's breasts rose and fell.

Swallowing hard, Quinn moved to her side. They had placed her arms over the covers, her hands at her sides. Reaching out, he slid his fingers beneath her right hand. How cool it felt! Anxiety filled him again.

Kerry's head was wrapped in white gauze. Her right temple, where the bullet had struck, was hidden beneath a dressing. How pale she looked! Moving closer, he stared down at her, grasping her hand more firmly and lifting it against his heart.

"Kerry? It's me, Quinn. I'm here, sweet pea. You're okay. You're going to make it. You hear me?" Gently, he grazed her wan cheek with his fingers. How dark her thick lashes looked against her flesh. She was warm and dry, but unmoving. Only the monitors beeping and clicking told him she was alive. A tube protruded from her open mouth, pumping oxygen systematically into her lungs. Quinn could barely stand it, seeing her like this.

Keeping her limp fingers clasped protectively in his, he ran his other hand caressingly up and down her forearm. "Listen to me," he said gruffly, "you're going to get well. The doctor put you into a coma on purpose. The bullet hit you in the side of the head, Kerry. It broke the bone, but that was all. Your brain is okay, just a little swollen is all." He could see where they had placed a dry-ice pack against that area to reduce any swelling. He knew that she was receiving steroids by IV to reduce the inflammation, as well.

The beeps and sighs continued, steady and unabated.

Closing his eyes, Quinn felt dizzy and scared. Even though they'd said that Kerry's chances of surviving were good, anything could happen. A sudden blood clot could form. She could have a massive cerebral hemorrhage and die. Sometimes Quinn wished he didn't know as much about emergency medical procedures as he did. In this case, his knowledge scared him. He knew the possibilities, and all of them were bad.

Opening his eyes, he leaned down and brushed his lips against her cheek, which felt like soft peach fuzz. Kissing her gently, he lifted his head a little and whispered, "Kerry, I love you. Don't ask me when or how it happened. But you being hurt like this, out of the blue, showed me the truth." His fingers tightened again around her cool, limp hand. "Sweet pea, just know I'll be here for you. Tomorrow, I don't know what will happen. I'm going to go now... I gotta go sleep. When I wake, I'll be back over here and we'll talk some more, okay? Just know I love you. And I always will...."

January 25: 1400

The world was swirling in shades of dark and light before Kerry's closed eyes. She felt herself whirling downward, growing heavier by the minute. Taking a deep, ragged breath, she struggled against the sensations. There were noises around her, and low voices, both male and female, nearby. Most of all, she could feel someone's warm, strong hand around hers, and it was wonderfully stabilizing to her in this netherworld she floated in.

"She's becoming conscious," Dr. Edmonds said,

with a smile at Quinn, who stood on the other side of the bed, holding Kerry's hand. "Excellent. We've stopped giving her drugs to keep her in a coma and she's coming out right on schedule. This is a good sign." Dr. Edmonds removed her stethoscope and placed it against Kerry's blue-gowned chest.

Quinn stood there, breath suspended momentarily. For seven days Kerry had been unconscious and on life support. He'd been out on duty in Area Five today when Morgan had sent for him, with news that Dr. Edmonds was going to awaken Kerry. The swelling in her brain was down. Everything looked good.

Dr. Edmonds, a U.S. Navy first lieutenant, straightened up and smiled slightly. "She's becoming conscious, Lieutenant Grayson. We'll leave now, but if you need anything, Nurse Williams here will assist you," she said, gesturing to the red-haired woman who stood beside her.

"Thanks," Quinn said sincerely. "For everything…"

Dr. Edmonds grinned and pushed her short black hair off her broad forehead. "My pleasure, Lieutenant. Just stay with your lady. Keep talking to her. It will bring her out more quickly."

When they'd left, Quinn turned and faced Kerry. The tube in her mouth had been removed. She was breathing well on her own. There were still two IVs, one in each arm, going into her veins and supplying her with life-giving nutrients.

"Sweet pea?"

The words echoed through Kerry's awakening senses. She knew that voice. And she knew that wonderful endearment. Quinn! Quinn was nearby. She heard the low, off-key tone close beside her. As she honed in on the sound, she could feel the soft tickle of his warm, moist breath against her ear.

When the corners of Kerry's mouth lifted slightly, Quinn's heart soared with unchecked joy. He leaned down and pressed a tender, welcoming kiss against her lips. Her mouth was chapped, and cool to his touch.

How much he'd missed Kerry! The last three days he'd been back in Area Five, preparing for the hunter-killer team that would be flown in shortly— a team whose sole focus would be to hunt down the Diablo and capture them once and for all.

"Hey, sweet pea. I'm here. It's Quinn. I've really missed you the last three days. I've been out in your neighborhood—Area Five. I brought back a whole bunch of handwritten notes from the folks who love you, Kerry. I've got them here with me. When you're fully awake, I want you to read them. Those people really care about you. Every day I get radio reports from Morgan about you—how you're doing and what's happening. And everyone wants to know the latest. There's a lotta people pullin' for you,

Kerry." His voice wobbled. "Especially me..." He squeezed her hand tenderly.

The brush of Quinn's lips against hers was the most wonderful sensation Kerry had ever experienced. Moments later, his voice, deep and steady, filled with love for her, brought her completely out of her coma state. Despite Kerry's fragmented senses, there was no question that Quinn loved her. She could feel it in the touch of his strong, warm hand around hers, in the butterfly kiss he'd brushed across her lips. She could hear it in his low voice.

Holding his breath, Quinn saw Kerry's lashes flutter once, twice, three times. As they slowly lifted, he saw the murky gray of her eyes as her gaze settled on him. The doctor had warned him that because of the drugs, she might be disoriented for a while, but talking to her, giving her information, would help her focus and respond.

Leaning down, he kissed her brow as it wrinkled slightly. "Welcome back, sweet pea. You're here with me. And you're safe. You're going to live, Kerry. Everything's gonna be fine. Believe me...." And he looked deeply into her eyes, no more than six inches away from his.

Drowning in the blazing blue of his narrowed eyes, Kerry felt her heart speed up with joy. Seeing the suffering, the anxiety in Quinn's face made her want to reach out and reassure him, but she was too weak to do that. Instead, she gave him a lopsided smile.

"Hi, stranger…"

"Hi…"

"I'm okay…." Kerry whispered, and closed her eyes. It took all her energy just to try and pull two thoughts together, then speak them.

"Yes, you are." Quinn struggled with the crazy jumble of emotions tunneling through him. "I want to yell and scream and shout to the world that you're okay," he told her. "There's so many people who have been praying for you, Kerry. Who want you to pull through. And you have." Lifting her hand, Quinn gently turned it over in his and kissed the back of it. "You're going to be fine."

His words were like healing balm to her spinning and slowly awakening senses. Kerry tried to close her fingers around his, but felt incredibly weak. Fragments of his words, of what he'd told her as she'd awakened, were floating loosely, like flotsam and jetsam in the ocean of her awareness.

Just her effort to try and squeeze his hand brought tears to Quinn's eyes. Gently touching her cheek, he stroked it with his fingertips. He could see her struggling to break the bonds of grogginess, to be here with him. "Easy, Kerry. Don't try so hard. Just take your time. I'm not going anywhere. I'll be here while you become conscious. Okay? Don't fight. Everything will slowly make sense to you over the next couple of hours, according to Dr. Edmonds."

Forcing her eyes open, she met his tender, burning look. Trying to speak, she found her voice was raspy from disuse. Her throat was sore and it hurt to talk.

"You? You're okay, Quinn? The shots? Diablo…"

Seeing the fear in her eyes, Quinn realized she was recalling the firefight. "Shh, sweet pea, I'm okay. I wasn't harmed. You were. You were shot twice. Once in the right thigh. The doc said it was just a flesh wound, and it's healing well. The second bullet hit you in the right side of your head. It cracked your skull, but you're going to be okay there, too. The doc said you'll probably have one helluva headache. Do you?"

She saw the care and concern in Quinn's eyes— and the exhaustion. "Yes… My head…it's killing me."

His response melted together. He was speaking too fast for her to grasp all the words. More than anything, she was relieved that he wasn't wounded. As a matter of fact, Quinn looked wonderful to her. He was in a clean uniform, and had recently shaved. His dark hair was short and combed. Still, he looked worried. About her.

"I'll get the nurse in here to give you more pain meds through the IV," he told her. Quinn started to leave, but her fingers tightened unexpectedly around his.

"No..." Kerry whispered.

Her cry tore at him. Halting instantly, he turned back to her, his hand strong and firm around hers. "I'm not going far," he reassured her. "I'm just going to get the nurse, Kerry. I'll be right back. I promise."

When Quinn saw tears welling up in her eyes, it ripped him apart. Teardrops fell from the corners of her eyes, leaking down toward her ears. Reaching out, he wiped the moisture away with his thumbs.

"Everything's okay, sweet pea. Really, it is. It's you I was worried about. The doc says you're gonna be fine."

Unable to stop the tears, Kerry clung to his darkening features. Quinn was visibly upset over her crying, she saw, but she couldn't help herself.

"I—I just..." She choked and swallowed despite her painful throat. When Quinn's warm hand settled against her cheek to give her solace, more tears fell.

"What?" Quinn whispered, his mouth near her ear. "What's wrong, Kerry?" He was alarmed, unsure of why she was crying. Was she in that much pain from her head wound? Or was it something else? Fear clawed at him. Was her health deteriorating?

Opening her eyes, his face blurring before her, Kerry choked out in a raspy voice, "I lost Lee. I—I can't...lose you...."

Chapter Nine

January 17: 0900

Quinn couldn't still his sense of urgency as he swung silently into the private room where they had placed Kerry late last night. She had rebounded remarkably, according to Dr. Edmonds, and they had desperately needed the ICU room for someone else in far worse shape than she was.

The sun was shining brightly through the partially opened venetian blinds, leaving stripes of sunlight across Kerry's bed.

"Hi!" He smiled at her warmly as he eased the door closed. "I see you're up, bright-eyed and bushy tailed."

Kerry managed a wan smile in return. She was

sitting up, with several pillows supporting her back. The orderly had just left her a tray with breakfast. "Bushy tailed?" she teased, her voice still raspy. Kerry had found out that the tube they'd put down her windpipe to help her breathe was the reason for the irritation in her throat. She was glad the tube was gone. Heart lifting, she smiled more widely. The entire room seemed to change, became lighter, and she felt happiness threading through her as he ambled toward her.

"Yeah, an old hill sayin'," he murmured. "It means you're looking real fine. Healthy."

"Mmm," Kerry said, "I'm better because you came to visit me."

Halting at her bedside, he eyed the tray resting on the moveable table across her lap. "I'm a sight for sore eyes, eh? Umm, breakfast. That's good. You need to eat and put a little meat on those bones." His mouth hitched upward.

The blue cotton gown was shapeless and hung on Kerry. Her hair was still hidden by the gauze wrapped around her head. But to him, she looked beautiful. Gazing deeply into her eyes, he saw some of the old life, those silver flecks, coming back into them.

Wrinkling her nose, Kerry offered him a slice of whole wheat bread that had already been buttered. "Want to share it with me?" As their fingers touched, she saw his blue eyes grow stormy with desire—for her.

"Thanks," he said, pulling up a chair and sitting down facing her, his right leg resting against the tubular frame of her bed. It was 0800—the earliest Quinn was allowed, by hospital rules, to visit. He'd gotten up early, shaved, showered and put on a pair of fresh cammos. No more would he take such mundane acts for granted. Being out in Area Five without water to shave or shower with had taught him that.

Kerry stirred the fork around in the fluffy scrambled eggs. She wasn't really hungry, but knew she had to eat.

"A sight for sore eyes," she said, giving him a glance. "That must be another hill saying?"

"Sure is. We have a whole other language in Kentucky."

Just being with Quinn was energizing for Kerry. She ate the eggs slowly and with relish. They actually tasted good. "I like all your expressions," she told him.

Munching on the toast, Quinn eyed Kerry closely. He didn't miss anything about her recovery. They'd already taken out one IV. She was on solid food. All those were good signs. "Stick around me," he teased, "and I'll teach you more." He wondered if she recalled what she'd said three days ago as she became conscious—about not wanting to lose him as she'd lost her husband. What did that mean? Quinn was afraid to read too much into it. Sometimes people with head injuries said a lot of things they either didn't recall later or didn't mean. Her words had meant the world to him, but the two of them barely knew each other. Their time together had been short and intense, but his heart didn't care. It wasn't at all reasonable when it came to Kerry.

"Is that a promise?" she whispered, setting the fork aside. How handsome Quinn looked. She could clearly see the desire, the care for her, in his eyes. Just the tenderness of his rough voice, the intimate tone he used with her, spoke volumes. Her heart skittered as he looked at her.

"Do you want it to be, Kerry?"

Unable to tear her gaze from his, she replied softly, "Yes..." And then she opened her hands in a helpless gesture. "I know we haven't known one another long, Quinn...."

Nodding, he set the piece of toast back on her tray. "Not long, but it's been pretty intense," he answered.

Touching her head carefully, Kerry said, "I've got a roaring headache, so I'm not going to be the best of company."

"Want me to get the nurse? Do you need a stronger pain med?" He was already halfway out of his chair.

"No...it comes and goes." Managing a slight

smile, Kerry admitted, ''When my heart starts beating hard and I get scared, my blood pressure rises and that's when the pain comes on. Dr. Edmonds told me that would happen at first. With time, as the bone mends, it will go away.''

''So, you need to do things to keep your blood pressure down?'' Her eyes were hauntingly beautiful to Quinn, so full of life. Right now, he was scared and tentative. Did Kerry want the same thing he did? He wasn't sure, and he was too much of a coward to ask. As a marine, he might be able to storm a rampart, but when it came to this, he felt frozen by the fear of possible rejection. He watched Kerry's mobile face, so open and readable.

''Life raises my blood pressure,'' she told him wryly, pushing the tray aside.

''You look worried. What's bothering you, Kerry?''

Quirking her mouth, she stared down at her hands clasped in her lap. ''I worry about Petula. Have you heard from her? From Sylvia? Are you in touch with them?''

''Yeah, they're both okay. I was in radio contact with Beau late last night, checking in with them to make sure everything was okay. They both miss you. Petula is getting regular MREs now, and so is Sylvia. They love the tent. The heat.'' He smiled. Just seeing the anxiety leave Kerry's eyes made him feel better.

"Good," she whispered fervently. "And what about Diablo? Are they still around? Or did they move into another area?"

Shrugging, Quinn said, "I don't know for sure. Morgan Trayhern is working on a plan to locate them. He realizes that my fire team can't respond as we first planned. And disease is starting to spread. He's trying to coordinate medical teams getting into our area to help stop the epidemics."

Kerry saw worry lurking in Quinn's darkening eyes. Frowning, she reached out, her fingers grazing his hand as it rested on the edge of her bed. "Are you going to be involved in getting the medical teams in there?"

Just the touch of her hand sent an ache straight to his heart. Quinn realized Kerry was a helluva lot braver than he was on the emotional front. She wouldn't touch him if he didn't mean something to her. The question was, how serious about him was she? The question almost tore out of him, but he couldn't find the guts to ask her yet.

"I don't know. I spent part of yesterday down at the brig facility going through mug shots, trying to ID the Diablo dudes we ran into. We wounded one of 'em and took out the others. The one that's still alive is here at the hospital right now, under armed guard. He didn't have any identification on him, and he's not talking to the military detectives put on the case."

Shivering, Kerry closed her eyes. "He's here?"

"Yeah." Quinn's fingers curled around her hand. "Don't worry, okay? That dude is going nowhere. The marines guarding him are brig chasers—and they're big and mean. They all hope he makes a break for it. They'd like nothing better than to take him down permanently after what he did to you." So would he, but Quinn knew it wasn't right. Let the legal system get this guy. He felt satisfaction in knowing the twenty-year-old-man was staring at a very long federal prison sentence for injuring and nearly killing Kerry. She was a law enforcement officer, and judges took a hard line and handed out long sentences to those who would do such a thing.

"I guess…well, I was wondering about him, too…." Sighing, she squeezed Quinn's hand. "I'm glad you're here with me. I'm feeling really vulnerable right now, shaky…. I was crying earlier. I don't know why, I just was…."

"Dr. Edmonds said with a head injury your emotions can go up and down like a roller coaster at first," he murmured soothingly, seeing the angst and turmoil in her eyes.

"I just didn't expect it."

"I'm here. I'll help you as much as I can, sweet pea." Quinn gave her a tender look and gripped her fingers tighter for a moment.

"I'm so glad…" Kerry's voice broke. Tears flooded her eyes and Quinn's face blurred again.

"You know, before you stepped into my life, I felt like the rug was jerked out from under me. I felt unstable and unsure, Quinn. But when you're with me, I feel okay. I feel like I'm going to get through all this hell on earth." Sniffing, she reached over and took a tissue from the box on the bedstand, dabbed her eyes and blew her nose.

"You've been through a lot, Kerry," he said, his voice a rasp. Watching her wipe the tears away made his heart ache. How badly he wanted to hold her. Just hold her. "And it's gonna take time for you to work through all the trauma. The shock. Getting shot at and injured just compounds it. Give yourself some breathing room, okay?"

Nodding, she gripped the tissue in her left hand. "It hasn't been all bad, Quinn. After all, I met you." Risking a glance, she saw his eyes narrow upon her. His mouth was thinned and set, as if he were bracing himself for whatever she might say.

"You just walked into my life and blew me away," Kerry told him brokenly. "I never realized how much of a load I was carrying by myself until you came and helped me out by sharing it. I liked your sensitivity, your care for others. I guess I had this stereotype in my head about rough, tough marines. When Morgan Trayhern told me you were coming, I wasn't thrilled pink about it, to be honest."

He grinned. "No?"

"No. I thought you'd be antiwoman or anti–law enforcement and just want to storm the beach and take over." She managed a shy smile as his grin widened.

"I respected what you'd done, Kerry. I saw how the people responded to you. I had no business coming in and trying to take over. We needed to learn from you, listen to you. And we did."

"I know." Shaking her head, she added, "Most of all, you were a wonderful leader, the best kind. I really liked working with you."

"You weren't what I expected, either," Quinn admitted. "I had a few stereotypes of my own to bury regarding you." He saw her answering smile.

Kerry was looking tired. Quinn knew she needed to sleep, so he got up and reluctantly released her hand. "Listen, you need to rest. Okay?"

Sighing, Kerry laid her head back on the pillows and closed her eyes. "I'm tired all of a sudden, Quinn." And she already missed his strong, warm hand on hers.

Walking around the bed, Quinn moved the wheeled table with the tray to one side. "Sleep, sweet pea," he whispered, leaning over and brushing a kiss on her wrinkled brow.

Opening her eyes, Kerry stared up into that blue gaze focused on her. "I feel so warm, safe and happy with you close to me like this...."

Reaching out, Quinn stroked her pale cheek.

"Then I'll make a habit of being a pest around here. I've got to meet Morgan in a few minutes. I'll come back late this afternoon and check on you."

Closing her eyes, she absorbed Quinn's touch like life-giving water to thirsty ground. "I'd like that...a lot...."

"I'll be back."

"Promise?"

"Promise."

January 28: 2100

Kerry looked at the clock on the wall; it was 2100. Darkness had fallen outside her private room. Most of her meal, which had been delivered at 1800, was still sitting there, untouched. Where was Quinn? There was a phone at her bedside, but she had no number to contact him. Worried, she kept glancing toward the door and then out the window.

There was a soft knock on the door and it opened.

"Quinn..."

He smiled tiredly and took off his cap. "Hi. Sorry I'm late. Things snowballed today." He shut the door behind him. Turning, he saw the anxiousness in Kerry's eyes even though she tried to hide her reaction.

"I'm just beginning to realize how busy it is around this base," she murmured. How good Quinn looked! But he was tired. She could see it in his eyes and the set of his mouth. He stuffed the cap he'd been wearing into his back pocket and unbuttoned his bulky jacket. Taking it off, he threw it on the chair next to her bed.

"Twenty-five hours a day," he assured her. Moving to her tray, he said, "What's this? You haven't touched your food. How come?" And he gave her a concerned look. There was a bit of color in her cheeks as he met and held her gaze. "Aren't you feeling any better?"

"I'm okay," Kerry lied. "I was just...well, worried when you didn't show up this afternoon...."

Moving the tray back across her bed, over her lap, Quinn opened the container of Jell-O and pulled off the transparent wrapper. "I got asked to fly out to Area Five unexpectedly, Kerry. At 1500 today. I'm sorry I couldn't let you know."

"I figured something came up." She watched as he picked up the spoon and handed her the container.

"You need to eat. Get your strength back, sweet pea."

Rallying at his undivided care, Kerry took the Jell-O and spooned some into her mouth. It was sweet and tasted good.

Unwrapping a sandwich, Quinn sat down on the edge of her bed and faced her.

"Help yourself," she said between bites. "I'm not that hungry."

"I'm a starvin' cow brute," he said with a chuckle. Just being with Kerry lifted his spirits. "That's hill slang for a steer." He saw her mouth draw into a smile. Did Kerry know how beautiful she was to him? Quinn didn't think so. He was ravenous and bit into the sandwich as she continued to daintily eat the strawberry Jell-O.

"Let me fill you in on the day's events," he told her between bites. There was some orange juice in a bottle, so he opened it and poured half of it into the plastic cup for her and kept half for himself.

"Morgan asked me to fly out on a Huey shipment bound for Area Five at 1500. Even though my fire team is there, and they have a new corporal, he wanted me to reconnoiter the area for the incoming medical team that will be here tomorrow evening. I spent all afternoon, until dark, going over a street map of the area, noting information that this team will need. There's all kinds of sickness starting to crop up. Dysentery, typhoid, strep, and others. Morgan is trying to get medical teams in there to stop it, but our medical supplies can't even begin to handle the epidemics that are starting to explode in the area."

"I've been worried sick about that, Quinn. I knew it would only be a matter of time. People are drinking dirty, unsafe water. They're eating food that's rotten and germy. I'm glad Morgan has made the medical teams a priority.'' She brightened a bit. ''Did you see Petula? Sylvia?''

Smiling, he nodded. ''The first thing I did when we landed was drop in for a visit with them. They're fine. They asked about you and I told you you're doing fine. Petula cried. But it was tears of happiness.''

Sighing, Kerry whispered, ''That's great.''

''You're missed by everyone,'' he told her seriously. ''Walking around the area, I must have had close to thirty people come up and ask me about you. They knew you'd been wounded and they were worried.''

''I lie here thinking about so many of them. I miss everyone. We bonded because of the tragedy and they feel like extended family to me now,'' Kerry said. She took a drink of orange juice.

''To them, you are family,'' he agreed. Quinn handed her half the turkey sandwich.

''Eat this.''

She bit into it without a word. Her spirits were flying. The darkness, the depression she was feeling, dissolved.

''I didn't run into Diablo, either,'' Quinn told her, frowning. ''I think the gunfight with us changed things. I'm not sure where they are right now.''

''Hiding, more than likely,'' Kerry answered. The turkey was amazingly tasty. She realized for the first time that she was truly famished. It had to be

Quinn's presence that triggered her appetite. With her leg resting against his hip where he sat on her bed, she sponged in his presence like the earth soaked up the rays of the warming sun. The happiness in his eyes made her heart beat harder. Hope threaded through Kerry, strong and good.

"Yeah, that's what Logistics thinks. Morgan is asking me to be point man on this project to try and find them."

Frowning, Kerry whispered, "Does that mean you'll go out with another team to find Diablo?"

"Take it easy," he said, wiping his mouth with a paper napkin after finishing his half of the sandwich. "No, I'm being assigned back to Area Five as Logistics officer." He smiled at her. "I'll be working with you—again." Kerry had made it clear she wanted to go back to her area. Dr. Edmunds agreed that she could as soon as her head wound was better. The flesh wound on her thigh was almost healed.

Shocked, Kerry stared at him. "Officer?" A thrill shot through Kerry. Quinn was going to be working with her once more. She felt euphoric.

Chuckling, Quinn said, "Did you notice the black embroidered bar on each of the shoulders of my shirt here?" He pointed to his left epaulet. The silver bars Morgan had given him would go on his official marine uniform, but not on his cammies. "I got a field commission, Kerry. It sure shocked me. That kind of thing hasn't been done since Vietnam. But Morgan said they were giving it to me because of the earthquake. They need more seasoned enlisted men and women out there in the basin. They're shorthanded and they need leaders to get the help to where it's critical. They don't have enough marine officers to do that with, so they're making new ones so we can help sooner, faster, better.''

"Oh, Quinn, congratulations!'' She reached out and touched his hand.

He grasped her fingers and squeezed them gently. "It was sure a surprise to me.''

"Well deserved, I'd say. What a gift.''

"You're my gift,'' he told her seriously. "In more ways than one, Kerry.'' He lifted her hand and pressed a kiss to the back of it. "All I want is for you to eat, sleep, rest and get better. The world might have fallen apart around us, but we have each other. That's the gift to me.'' He hoped it was for her, too, but he wasn't about to put words into her mouth on that topic. Just the way her eyes turned smoky with desire made his heart beat faster. The way her soft, full lips parted made him groan inwardly.

Kerry didn't want Quinn to release her hand, but he did. He was intent on getting her to eat. Uncovering a piece of chocolate cake with a thin layer of white frosting, he divided it between them, then handed her the fork.

"At some point when the time's right," Kerry told him softly, "we need to sit down and do some serious talking, Quinn."

His heart thudded in his chest. Looking down, he muttered, "Yeah, I know. Things have been crazy of late, and our worlds have been like sheets twisted in a windstorm."

"I love your hill sayings," Kerry said. More than anything, she loved him. And how she felt had to be put on the table. Whether Quinn loved her, she didn't know, and that scared her as little else had in her life. Still, Kerry knew she had to tell Quinn how she felt.

"Two days from now," he told her, "if things go right, let's talk. Okay? I'll be back on base on the thirtieth."

Nodding, she picked disinterestedly at the cake. "Yes, two days, Quinn." Her appetite had fled once more with the fear of losing Quinn. His larger-than-life presence was exactly that—something so good, clean and wonderful that Kerry had a tough time believing that life had placed a second good man before her.

Chapter Ten

January 30:1600

Quinn hurried into the greenhouse that was attached to the hospital. Laura Trayhern had told him that in the last two days, Kerry had become mobile in a wheelchair. Her recovery was so swift that she was spending a lot of time in the greenhouse instead of staying in her room.

He hadn't realized there was a greenhouse and solarium affixed to the hospital. It was a nice way to get the patients out of their rooms. His heart hammered. Would Kerry be glad to see him? That he'd promised her he'd see her two days ago made his gut clench. Would she understand? Pushing through the double doors, their windows steamed up because of the humidity, he entered a world of warmth and moisture.

The greenhouse was a glass-and-steel structure housing a good five thousand square feet of tropical greenery—brightly flowering orchids and tall palms that reached for the light. Where was Kerry? Quinn halted and looked around. The redbrick sidewalk was wide enough to support a wheelchair. Very few people were in the exquisite greenhouse, maybe because it was 1600. Mouth dry, he wiped it with the back of his hand and turned. Something told him to take the left fork in the path, around the huge stand of palms in the red planter that welcomed visitors into this jungle world.

He found Kerry at the end of the curving red path, a watering pot in her hands. She was watering some of the low plants along the sidewalk, one at a time. From where he stood, he could see that she wore only a dressing on her temple, and the swathes of gauze around her head had been removed. Her hair, dark and slightly curled, had been recently washed and framed her face. Most surprising, she was in civilian clothes and not a hospital gown. Kerry wore a long-sleeved, pale pink turtleneck that provocatively outlined her upper body. She had small, beautiful breasts, Quinn realized for the first time. When she'd been in her uniform or wearing a flak vest, that feminine secret had been hidden from him. Further, the jeans she wore outlined her long, curved thighs. She was leaning down, a peaceful look on her face as she dribbled water on a bright red anthurium with dark green foliage.

"I'm kinda thirsty," Quinn said, coming forward. "Can I get a drink of water from you, too?"

Kerry's head snapped to the left. Quinn's voice was low, intimate and teasing. As she sat up, she nearly dropped the watering device.

"Quinn!" Her voice was muffled by the many plants and high humidity around them. She twisted toward him. Her heart bounded and joy shot through her. He was grinning crookedly, a welcome burning in his eyes.

With a soft cry, Kerry set the watering bucket down and turned the wheelchair toward him. The look of happiness on his darkly bearded face, in his bloodshot eyes, made her smile.

Quinn crouched before her, his hands settling on her shoulders. "Hi, stranger."

"Hi, yourself." Kerry touched his bearded face. There was dirt on the side of his jaw, and his cammies were dirty, also. "And you're no stranger."

"No?" He searched her silver-flecked eyes. There was no doubt Kerry was happy to see him. He ran his hands across the silky pink turtleneck covering her shoulder and upper arms. More than anything, he liked touching Kerry. Her body was firm and athletic.

"No. How are you?" To heck with it. Kerry

threw her arms around him and drew him against her in a tight, quick embrace. Quinn came forward without protest, chuckling as he wrapped his strong arms carefully around her shoulders and held her. He smelled of sweat. Kerry knew he'd been out in the field for two days in Area Five.

"I'm fine—now." Giving her a quick kiss on her ruddy cheek, Quinn eased away. Taking off his cap, he rose and tucked it in a back pocket. "You look great." *Delicious.* He wanted her. So very badly. He wanted to claim her in every way to show her how much she meant to him.

"Thanks." Kerry laughed delightedly. Gesturing to the brick walk, she said, "Can you sit down? Do you have a minute or are you off putting out another brushfire crisis somewhere else?"

Sitting on the sidewalk, which was only slightly damp, Quinn crossed his legs and looked up at her. "I'm sorry I couldn't be here this morning when I said I would, Kerry. I know I promised." He opened his hands in a helpless gesture.

"Don't worry about it," she murmured. "Morgan came by and told me that Diablo attacked again in Area Five and that he ordered you to stay out in the field with another squad to help protect the people."

Grimacing, Quinn ran his fingers through his short, dark hair. "Yeah. We got there before they did any real damage."

"Everyone safe?" Hungrily, Kerry absorbed his

exhausted features. All she wanted to do right now was lie with him, hold him and let him know that she loved him. But it was still too soon for that, she knew.

"Yeah. They took off just as we landed in the Huey. The people were shaken up, but okay."

"Morgan said the medical teams were delayed?"

"I'm afraid so. Flight schedules are being juggled all the time because of high-priority needs. Right now, medicine is not the top dawg, but Morgan's trying to make it so."

"Why not?" Anger moved through her. "I heard cholera is breaking out all over the place," she said, trying to curb her frustration. Cholera was a deadly disease found in squalid third world countries, not the U.S.A. It shocked Kerry to realize that it was here now, only miles away from the base. That living conditions out there were worsening daily.

"Water and food still have top billing but Logistics are trying to get the medical teams in there, thanks to Morgan pushin' his weight around to get them prioritized," Quinn said with a slight smile. He saw the worry etched on Kerry's face. "Good news, though. Petula is fine, as is Sylvia and everyone you know back in Area Five. They said to send their hellos to you."

Brightening, Kerry sighed. "Oh, good! You know, deep down in my heart, Quinn, I'm a big worrywart."

Chuckling, he said, "I know." Reaching out, he captured her hand with his larger one. "Listen," he said, his voice dropping to a rough growl, "we need to talk. I need to level with you. I'm scared to do it, afraid of the outcome, but I owe you that, Kerry. And I owe it to myself."

She curled her fingers around his, light upon dark. The back of Quinn's hand was hairy; hers was white and smooth. Heart pumping violently for a moment, she licked her lips and gravely met his narrowing blue gaze.

"I know... I've got to come clean, too. And I'm scared, if that makes you feel any better?" One corner of her mouth curved upward. She saw some of the tension in his face ease. Just her touching him was helping Quinn's distress. That realization was wonderful to Kerry. Touch, for her, was so important and so healing.

"Okay, sweet pea...should I go first?"

"Yeah," Kerry said wryly, "I'm too scared. Brave ones go first."

Snorting softly, Quinn leaned over and pressed a small kiss to the back of her hand, which was warm now, not chilled as it had been days ago. "I'm a coward over matters of the heart," he confided. "But here goes...." And he took in a ragged breath and let it out.

"When you got hit out there in the field, Kerry,

something I'd been avoiding since I met you broke loose and hit me right between the runnin' lights, in the middle of my forehead. When I ran to your side after the firefight, I thought you were dead. I was so scared. Scared to death. I remember the thought howling inside my head and heart—that this wasn't fair. I'd just met you…thought so much of you… was attracted to you. This couldn't be happening!''

Gazing deeply into his troubled eyes, Kerry whispered, "So you liked me a little?"

Lifting his other hand, he grazed her flaming cheek. "That's an understatement…."

"I see…."

Unsure, Quinn searched her warm gray eyes, which grew lustrous at his halting admittance. Fear ate at him. He had to go on, had to be honest with her. "I didn't go into Area Five expecting to meet a woman I'd be drawn to. I didn't know what to expect, Kerry, but I didn't expect how I'd feel about you." He ran his fingers lightly down her arm and allowed them to come to rest on top of her small, slender hand.

"I got burned real bad in a relationship a couple of years ago. The gal turned on me after I asked her to marry her. I found out then that she wanted an officer. She was a social climber. She didn't want some lowly lance corporal in the Marine Corps. As soon as some green lieutenant right out of the Naval

Academy made eyes at her, she started chasing him and let me go.''

''I'm so sorry,'' Kerry said. She saw the anger and hurt in his expression. ''That must have been awful. You were sincere. She wasn't.''

''Exactly.'' Quinn stared down at Kerry's hand for a moment. ''So, when I met you, I wasn't expecting to...well, fall for you like that....''

His mouth was working, his brows were knitted and he wasn't meeting her gaze. Kerry could feel him wrestling within himself. Gently, she whispered, ''Quinn, I wasn't expecting to fall in love with you, either, but I have.''

The words landed like bombs and exploded within him. Jerking his chin up, he saw Kerry smiling softly, tears glistening in her wide, doelike eyes.

''You—love me?''

''Yes. Don't ask me how or when it happened.'' She gave a half laugh and shook her head. ''I sure wasn't looking for a man, Quinn. After losing Lee, I knew the universe wasn't going to put a second good man in front of me.'' Her smile fading, Kerry choked out the words. ''But they did. They gave me you, Quinn.''

Sitting very still, he digested her tearful words. Kerry loved him. It took long, precious seconds for that realization to really sink into his wildly beating heart. Unable to catch his breath, he sat there, her hand enclosed in his, their gazes clinging together in the warmth and humidity and peace of the silent greenhouse.

Kerry had more courage than he did, Quinn realized. She'd admitted her love for him first. Getting up on one knee and cupping her shoulders, he said in a rasp, "And I've fallen in love with you…and I don't know how or when or why, either. I just know I have, Kerry."

There, the truth. The unvarnished reality of how he felt was out. He saw his awkward words touch Kerry, saw the joy leap in her sparkling gray eyes. His hands tightened for a moment on her shoulders as she raised her own hands to frame his face.

"I'm scared, Quinn. Scared to death to feel like I do toward you."

"Me, too. It's the wrong place, Kerry. The wrong time. Bad timing."

"Either of us could get killed out there in the line of duty. I almost died already. In another week, I'm going home, back to Area Five, to carry on my work there."

His hands squeezed her shoulders, firm and loving. "I know you're goin' back there. Morgan already told me."

"You'll be with me, right?" She simmered with joy and with fear as she drowned in his aqua gaze, which was filled with love toward her.

"Every moment, sweet pea. I'm not lettin' you out of my sight. We'll work that area together.

That's what Morgan has in mind—a melding of military and civilian law enforcement to hold the fabric of the place together. With both of us back there, I know we can stabilize it."

"Together," Kerry said, "like the good team we've become."

"I want to kiss you...."

She smiled tenderly. "I'd like nothing better, Quinn. I need you...." And she did. Leaning forward, she met his descending mouth. His breath was warm and moist, flowing against her cheek as he moved his lips adoringly across hers. There was such restraint in him, as if she were a priceless vase that would shatter if he put too much stress on it.

"I won't break," she whispered against his mouth, and smiled as she opened her eyes and met his gaze.

Feeling her lips curve in a smile, Quinn eased away momentarily. "You're strong, sweet pea. Strong and beautiful and every inch the kind of woman I've always dreamed of, but never thought I would meet."

Laughing softly with happiness, Kerry slid her fingertips across his hard jawline to his thickly corded neck. "Then kiss me silly...! I really need you, Quinn. You make me feel safe and warm and good all at the same time...."

Not wanting to disappoint her, Quinn eased his hands across her jaw and tilted her head just slightly to take full advantage of her smiling mouth. This time, he moved his lips against hers with a deep, searching abandon. Her breathing became chaotic. Her hands ranged restlessly against his neck and shoulders as he tasted her, cajoled her and made her a part of him as never before.

His lower body burned hotly, with almost a painful cramping sensation, he wanted her so badly. Yet Quinn knew the time wasn't right, at least not yet. They'd barely met. They needed the coming weeks and months to get to know one another better. As he glided his mouth against hers, tasted her and inhaled her special feminine fragrance, Quinn sensed they'd both know when that time came.

Lost in the explosive heat and exploration of his strong male mouth against her softer lips, Kerry sighed. Quinn was powerful without being hurtful. As he caressed her head, her neck and shoulders, as if committing it all to memory, Kerry felt as if she were the most adored person on the face of the earth. How badly she wanted Quinn in all ways. Because of the past, she needed time to say a final farewell to Lee before she embarked on a new path with this incredible man who now held her so carefully and lovingly.

Easing back, Kerry gazed up at Quinn. His shoulders were so broad and capable, and he was so near to her, so solid and warm. "I never expected this, Quinn...not now, not ever...."

Sliding his hands across her shoulders and down her arms, to capture her hands in her lap, Quinn sat back on his boot heels. His heart was thudding with longing, his chest expanding with joy. The happiness burning in Kerry's eyes was real, and it made him feel good about himself as a man.

"I didn't either, Kerry. Maybe that's why it'll work for us in the long run."

Nodding, she ran her tongue over her lower lip. Kerry liked the taste of Quinn. Her mouth tingled in the wake of his branding, capturing kiss. Trying to catch her breath, she managed a small, wry smile. "I need the time. I think you already know that."

"Yeah, I do. I'm willing to wait, Kerry. Good things are always worth waiting for, my ma says."

"Your ma is right," she laughed breathlessly. Holding his hands, she absorbed his gentleness toward her.

"We have a lot of work in front of us. And danger." Quinn's brow became furrowed for a moment. "It's gonna take months before the L.A. basin gets back on a stable footing. And it's gonna get worse before it gets better. Morgan was saying that they're now entering the critical phase, where disease is going to begin to kill off thousands of people."

Sadness settled in Kerry's heart. She looked around the quiet, empty greenhouse, breathed the fragrant perfume of orchids in bloom. "I know. I feel guilty even being here. Every time I eat a meal,

I think of the thousands of people out there who are near starvation. It's a horrible thing, and I feel so frustrated that I can't change it or fix it."

"Nothing is gonna be a quick fix out there, Kerry." He reached forward and grazed the right side of her rib cage below her breast. "You need to put more weight on you before you go back out in the field, too. If you aren't strong and physically in shape, you can't help in ways you need to. You know that."

Hanging her head, she whispered, "I do know. It's just—hard, is all."

"That's one of the many things I love about you, sweet pea," he told her in a low, tender tone. "Your care of others. Your concern. You were feeding Petula what little food you could find, instead of yourself, I know."

"Can't fool you, can I?" Kerry's laugh was tinged with sadness.

Shaking his head, Quinn said, "No, you can't. You wear your heart, a heart as big as the mountains I was born in, on your sleeve, Kerry." He squeezed her fingers gently. "I love you."

Reaching out, she touched Quinn's sandpapery jaw and held his stormy blue gaze. "And I love you, too, Quinn. I'm glad we have the time. We'll learn more and more about each other as we work together out there. I like that. I'm looking forward to being with you again. I miss you not being around."

Kerry allowed her fingers to drop from his hard jaw, and gazed around her. "I'm lonely without you. I like hearing what you think, learning from your hill experience, about your life...."

"Every day I'm out there," Quinn told her in a quiet voice, "I'm lonely without you near me, Kerry. I feel like I'm half a person. You complete me in a way I've never been completed before. It scares me, but it also makes me feel good."

"Let's be scared together," Kerry suggested. "Life is in chaos right now. But we have one another. We have more than most. Even out of this terrible, escalating disaster, some good has come— I found you. I fell in love with you. And it's the best thing that's ever happened to me."

Epilogue

February 1: 0600

Quinn sat next to Kerry in Morgan Trayhern's cramped office. Logistics was in high gear since the cholera epidemic had started. They each had cups of steaming coffee in their hands as Morgan sat down across from them, his brow deeply furrowed. Quinn could see the man wasn't sleeping much; his eyes were bloodshot and shadowed with exhaustion.

Feeling for their leader, Quinn said, "Sir? Could you use a cup of coffee to jump-start your morning?" It was 0600, and the sky outside the open venetian blinds behind Morgan's desk was still dark.

"What?" Morgan lifted his head from riffling through several files on his desk.

"Coffee, sir? Can I pour you a cup?"

A vague smile twisting his mouth, Morgan said, "No, thanks... I've been up since 0400, Quinn, and if I have any more coffee, my nerves are going to start shrieking."

Kerry glanced over at Quinn. Today was her first day back on the job. Her leg was healed up sufficiently, but not fully. She'd battled hard to get back out to Area Five instead of languishing here at Camp Reed. Part of her felt guilty for taking up bed space, and eating so well when starvation was rampant in the L.A. basin now. Another part of her ached to be back with the people she worried about constantly. With Quinn and his fire team going back with her, she felt elated and hopeful.

"Well," Morgan muttered, locating the file he wanted, "finally..." He pulled it open and flattened it on his desk with his large hands. Outside his partially opened door, the office was thrumming. People were walking quickly up and down the gleaming passageway. Everyone was in a hurry. Time had run out on them. People were dying not by tens or twenties now, but by hundreds. Those numbers would reach the thousands soon if Morgan didn't get things in place pronto.

Thumping the file with his index finger, he told Quinn, "I've finally managed to get medical teams on the priority list. With word coming back daily from the helicopter flights out there, the feds are finally realizing we have an epidemic about to blow up in our face."

"That's great news, sir. At least about the medics."

"Yes, yes, it is." Scowling, Morgan rummaged around on his messy desk again. "Kerry?"

"Yes, sir?"

"We're going to get the first medical team, Alpha, into your area."

Clapping her hands, Kerry whispered, "Thank you!"

"Don't be so overjoyed," Morgan growled. "Your area has more epidemics than any other. Cholera, typhoid, salmonella... People are drinking whatever water they can find, and it's dirty and tainted. We're losing a lot of infants and children."

Glumly, Kerry nodded. "I understand, sir. Still, having a medical team sent in brings hope, and that's what the people need. They need to see the government working for them."

"It does..." he groused, frowning "...eventually. When enough pressure hangs over their heads. I'd like to put a few of those overweight senators and congressmen into the basin. They'd squall like scalded cats if they were deprived of their bread and butter for more than a day."

Quinn snorted. "There's no bread or butter left in the basin, sir."

"Exactly my point."

Kerry saw the frustration in Morgan's face. Having talked with Laura, she understood his barely veiled anger. Morgan had single-handedly fought red tape right up to the president to get medical teams put on a higher priority status. More than most people in the higher echelons of federal government, Morgan knew about disease. He knew it from his time spent in Vietnam, and then in the French Foreign Legion. He'd seen deprivation, starvation and disease in Southeast Asia and in Africa. And because of his experience, he knew what would happen in the quake zone.

"I'm sending in a reconnaissance team, Quinn, to work with the first medical team. I've managed to snag Dr. Samantha Andrews, a U.S. Navy doc, to help create crisis intervention teams. She's going out with two nurses and two enlisted orderlies to see if they can start combating the epidemic."

Sitting up a little straighter, Quinn smiled. "You're puttin' a Recon team with a medical unit?"

"I have to," Morgan muttered. "If I don't, and that medical team mixes up with Diablo, they could be murdered. No, I pulled strings to get this Recon unit pulled out of Kosovo and brought here to guard them."

"That's a good idea, sir."

"You know Lieutenant Roc Gunnison? He's the officer heading up this Recon team."

"A little," Quinn said. "He was here at Camp

Reed, and my team worked together with his from time to time before he was ordered overseas."

"What kind of man is he, Son? And don't be PC—politically correct—okay? I need the goods on this man because he's going to have to interface with Dr. Andrews. I know her. She's a strong, capable woman with a lot of guts and common sense. That's why I chose her to help create these med teams. She'll see what's wrong and know how to fix it to make the unit smoother and more reactive to the demands placed upon it."

Nodding, Quinn said, "I'm sure you have Captain Gunnison's file there?"

"Yes, I do. I happen to know his father, a very rich man who owns a computer company. Roc is a ring knocker."

"Ring knocker" was a term used for those who had graduated from Annapolis, a rarefied place where only the best navy and Marine Corps officers were chosen to go for an education. Quinn said, "He's the paramedic on his team, sir. And he's very good at what he does."

"His men like him?"

"They respect him, sir."

Grimacing, Morgan muttered, "Great." There was a fine line between like and respect. Morgan was hoping that this officer was the type of leader a team would go to hell and back for. Quinn carefully using the word respect spoke volumes, and not in Roc's favor. Scowling, Morgan rasped, "Okay, you've met Dr. Andrews?"

"Yes, sir, I have. She's a human dynamo."

Morgan saw Quinn brighten and sit up even straighter. He also saw the gleam of respect in the man's eyes for the woman doctor. Sam Andrews was a one-woman tornado in the hospital. She'd brought the facility up to speed to meet the overwhelming crisis they'd had to deal with when the quake victims started being flown in. She had been responsible for a lot of triage ideas and changes that affected the way patients were brought in and handled at the understaffed facility. She had saved lives by looking at the larger picture, and then making the necessary tweaks and adjustments that made the medical unit more responsive to the needs of the avalanche of incoming patients. Morgan liked her a lot.

"Okay, what's Gunnison's problem, Quinn? And be damned straight with me. I don't have time to pussyfoot on this one."

"Yes, sir. You know the saying, 'pride goeth before a fall'?"

Rolling his eyes, Morgan muttered, "Yes, unfortunately."

"That about sums it up, sir."

"He's pigheaded. He can't admit he's wrong?"

"Yes to both of those, sir."

"Great...!"

"He's very competitive, sir. But that's not a bad thing, usually...."

Nostrils flaring, Morgan glared across the desk at Quinn, who had an apologetic look on his face. "Except, if I'm reading between the lines on this one, your evaluation is that Dr. Andrews and Captain Gunnison are going to get along like oil and water."

"Uh...maybe like cats and dogs?"

"You've made my day, Lieutenant."

"I'm sorry, sir."

"Don't apologize." He shut the file dejectedly.

"I've seen a lot of Dr. Andrews," Kerry said, hope in her tone. "She's tough, sir. Firm and tough. I don't think she'll let this Recon officer run over her."

"Oh," Morgan chuckled, "I know she won't. Sam—er, Dr. Andrews, doesn't suffer fools lightly." He gave them a brief smile. "Thanks for your input. Both of you. Are you ready for your 0700 flight back home, Kerry?"

She smiled. "More than ready, sir. Thanks for all you've done to help them—and me. You're an angel in my eyes. A guardian angel of the best kind."

Morgan tapped his head. "Yeah? Well, I got a lot of people cursing at me and thinking I'm the devil incarnate back East in the Capital. I've been raising more hell. They're so tired of me that they're actually starting to give me what I want for these poor folks in the quake zone.''

Kerry wanted to stand up and hug Morgan. He looked like he could use a hug about now. She'd realized from further talks with Quinn that Morgan was like a one-man army on behalf of all the people out there in the L.A. basin. He was truly a knight in shining armor in her eyes.

Rising, Quinn smiled down at Kerry. ''You ready?''

She moved gingerly. Although healing, her head injury was still on the mend. Even now, Kerry moved carefully and not with her usual confidence. ''More than ready.''

Morgan lifted his hand. ''Stay in close touch. And expect that medical unit in tomorrow, possibly the day after. My people will be in radio contact with you about it.''

''Yes, sir,'' Quinn said, and he opened the door for Kerry.

Out in the passageway, they hugged the wall to avoid the stream of human traffic. Like a well-oiled machine, the Logistics department hummed in high gear twenty-four hours a day, with three shifts of people working at top speed.

Quinn opened an exit door for Kerry. There were no elevators in the building, and she would have to take the concrete steps slowly and carefully so as not to jar her head. He moved to her side. They were alone now, and he slipped his hand beneath her left elbow to steady her.

"Thanks," she whispered, looking up with a soft smile. Her heart swelled with such love for Quinn. Over the past week, now that their love was out in the open, their feelings had grown stronger, more beautiful and deeper. She cherished his touch, though it didn't come often enough. Out in the real world, they had to act with decorum and restraint. Touching or kissing wasn't allowed, unfortunately.

As she slowly took each step, Quinn at her side, Kerry said, "Do you think Dr. Andrews is going to get along with Captain Gunnison?"

Snorting, Quinn said, "No. That's like putting a fox and a chicken in the henhouse together."

"Who's the hen? Who's the fox?"

Laughing, Quinn said, "I don't know, sweet pea." He gave her a warm look. "But we'll be there to see it happen."

"My money's on Dr. Andrews. She's an amazon. A real Princess Xena."

"Roc Gunnison is nothin' to mess with, though," he pointed out. "When he thinks he's right, he'll move heaven and hell to prove it."

"Well," Kerry said dryly, "let's keep score. They're supposed to set up a medical tent city near our place at the shopping center, so we'll get fifty-yard seats to watch the battle of the titans."

His fingers closed around her elbow and he leaned

over and gave her a swift kiss on the cheek. "What kind of a bet do you want to place on them?"

Her skin tingled pleasantly where he'd kissed her, and she smiled at him. "My money's on the doctor."

"Okay, I'll back Roc."

"You marines *always* stick together."

Chuckling, Quinn said, "Yeah, I know...."

"I love you anyway."

"Whew, that's good to know!" And they laughed together as they started down the second flight of stairs on the way to their new life together.

* * * * *

Next month, look for
PROTECTING HIS OWN
when
MORGAN'S MERCENARIES:
ULTIMATE RESCUE
continues in the
Silhouette Intimate Moments line!
Only from USA TODAY
bestselling author
LINDSAY McKENNA
Turn the page for a sneak preview....

Chapter 1

Heart pounding, Sam watched the desert-colored Humvee approach at high speed. As it drew close, Sam could see Captain Roc Gunnison in the passenger seat. Lips tightening, she tried to gird herself as he stared at her flatly through the window of the vehicle. There was no welcome in those eyes. Only hardness.

Trying to appear nonchalant, she watched as the door of the Humvee opened and her nemesis stepped out. Her heart thumped again as she studied his hard, unyielding profile.

At thirty-two years of age, Gunnison was a seasoned marine who had seen action not only in Somalia, but in Kosovo, and he was highly decorated. Medium-boned, he appeared strong, capable and athletic in his desert cammos. His black hair was close-cropped and barely visible beneath the helmet he wore. Those eaglelike blue eyes, the color of the Montana sky she'd been born under, got to her.

As he swung his head in her direction, Sam's heart thundered briefly. Their eyes met and locked. Sam felt naked and vulnerable beneath his glacial assessment. Under any other circumstances, she'd find him a handsome man, with that square face and those craggy looks stamped with experience and lined from hours spent out in the elements. Now she found herself staring almost hungrily back at him. She knew it had to be the pressure she was under. Because experience had shown her that Roc was *not* the kind of man she wanted. Not on this mission. And not as a woman.

Roc couldn't tear his gaze from Dr. Andrews as she stood outside the helicopter in her U.S. Navy regulation clothing. Despite the desert-colored flak jacket that covered her upper body, he knew she was large boned and curvy beneath that mannish clothing she had to wear. He tried to glare at her, to let her know silently that he wasn't going to take any crap from her on his mission. Yet as the early morning breeze lifted her red hair away from her long, oval face and he saw her green eyes glittering with intelligence, Roc remembered this wasn't just any woman he was dealing with.

As he stared at her across the distance, he saw her lips part slightly. That was his undoing, dammit.

He groaned inwardly. Why did Andrews have to have such a soft, full mouth?

Scowling, Roc shut the door on the Humvee. Girding himself, he hefted his pack in one hand, his M-16 in the other, and stepped around the vehicle.

"Nice to see you again, Lieutenant," he drawled.

"Liar."

Stunned, Roc took a second look at her as he threw his pack into the cargo bay of the helo. "Excuse me?"

Sam met and held his surprised gaze. "You're a liar, Captain Gunnison. And don't try and sweet-talk me because it won't work. I call a spade a spade."

So much for her soft mouth. Lips tightening, Roc stared at her. "Okay, Lieutenant, have it your way. I was just trying to be social."

"Yeah, right. I saw the look you gave me. I know where I stand with you on this mission."

He glared down at her. "We need to talk. But not here. And not now. Once we get to Area Five, you and I are going to chat. Alone."

Giving him a cutting smile, Sam said, "Fine with me, Captain. Because frankly, you're the *last* man on earth I'd ever want to have with me on a mission."

After lobbing that grenade, Sam brushed by him and leaped up into the cargo bay of the helicopter. She found her nylon seat against the bulkhead and sat down, watching as Gunnison moved lithely into the hold and sat down on the opposite side. The load master slid the door shut and it locked.

Sam couldn't steady her fluttering heart. She felt like she'd been in combat, the way her adrenaline was pumping through her veins. If Gunnison thought he could run over her or intimidate her with just a look, he was badly mistaken. Judging from the frustration she saw on his face as he strapped in, she was sure he had gotten her message. She smiled to herself. This was her mission. People needed her and her team's help.

There was no way she'd let her tension with Gunnison get in the way of that.

If you enjoyed what you just read,
then we've got an offer you can't resist!

Take 2 bestselling love stories FREE!
Plus get a FREE surprise gift!

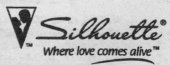

$ **Saving Money** $
Has Never Been
This Easy!

**Just fill out and send in this form from any
October, November and December 2002 books
and we will send you a coupon booklet worth a
total savings of $20.00 off future purchases of
Harlequin and Silhouette books in 2003.**

Yes! It's that easy!

**I accept your incredible offer!
Please send me a coupon booklet:**

Name (PLEASE PRINT)

Address   Apt. #

City   State/Prov.   Zip/Postal Code

**In a typical month, how many
Harlequin and Silhouette novels do you read?**

❏ **0-2**   ❏ **3+**

097KJKDNC7   097KJKDNDP

Please send this form to:
In the U.S.: Harlequin Books, P.O. Box 9071, Buffalo, NY 14269-9071
In Canada: Harlequin Books, P.O. Box 609, Fort Erie, Ontario L2A 5X3

Allow 4-6 weeks for delivery. Limit one coupon booklet per household. Must be
postmarked no later than January 15, 2003.

© 2002 Harlequin Enterprises Limited   PHQ402

SILHOUETTE *Romance*

COMING NEXT MONTH

#1624 SKY FULL OF PROMISE—Teresa Southwick
The Coltons
Dr. Dominic Rodriguez's fiancée ran out on him—and it was all
Sky Colton's fault! Feeling guilty about the breakup, Sky reluctantly
posed as Dom's fiancée to calm his frazzled mother. But would their
pretend engagement lead to a real marriage proposal?

#1625 HIS BEST FRIEND'S BRIDE—Jodi O'Donnell
Bridgewater Bachelors
Born in the same hospital on the same day, Julia Sennett, Griff Corbin
and Reb Farley were best friends—until romance strained their bonds.
Engaged to Reb, Julia questioned her choice in future husbands. Now
Griff must choose between his childhood buddy…and the woman he
loves!

#1626 STRANDED WITH SANTA—Janet Tronstad
Wealthy, successful rodeo cowboy Zack Lucas hated Christmas—he
didn't want to be a mail-carrying Santa and he certainly didn't want to
fall in love with Jenny Collins. But a brutal Montana storm left Zack
snowbound on his mail route, which meant spending the holidays in
Jenny's arms...!

#1627 THE BARON & THE BODYGUARD—Valerie Parv
The Carramer Legacy
Stricken with amnesia, Mathiaz de Marigny didn't remember telling
his beautiful bodyguard that he loved her—or that she had refused him.
Now Jacinta Newnham vowed a new start between them. But what
would happen when the truth surrounding Mathiaz's accident—and Jacinta's connection to it—surfaced?

#1628 HER LAST CHANCE—DeAnna Talcott
Soulmates
Looking for a spirited filly with unicorn blood, foreign heiress
Mallory Chevalle found no-nonsense horse breeder Chase Wells.
According to legend, his special horse could heal her ailing father and
restore harmony to her homeland. But could a love-smitten Mallory
heal Chase's wounded heart?

#1629 CHRISTMAS DUE DATE—Moyra Tarling
Mac Kingston was a loner who hadn't counted on sharing the holidays—
or his inheritance—with very beautiful, very wary and very pregnant
Eve Darling. But when she realized she'd found the perfect father—
and husband!—could she convince Mac?

SRCNM1002